SMALL HOURS

TRACY BROEMMER

Small Hours

By

Tracy Broemmer

Women's Fiction

Published by Tracy Broemmer

Edited by Lexie Broemmer

Cover Photo: Deposit Photos

Cover Design: Redbird Designs

For my family
All of you

I'll never forget
our holiday celebrations
through the years

1

Makenna

THE HOUSE AT THE CORNER OF TWELFTH AND MACLEAN always speaks to her when she drives by, but never more so than at Christmas time. Makenna Hodges cranes her neck to look at the wreath on the massive oak door. The house itself is heading toward a sorry state, but she imagines it was once really something to see.

She cranks the heat down as she brakes at the next corner. She'd forgotten to take her coat off when she left the house, and she's starting to sweat. No doubt Angie would make some snide comment about age and hormones if she were here. Makenna laughs anyway and reminds herself to call Angie later. They'd talked about getting their families together for dinner over the coming weekend, but they hadn't made definite plans.

Still hot, Makenna cracks her window and automatically reaches to turn down her music. Maybe no one else wants to hear Bing Crosby singing "The Holly and The Ivy" in November. Again, she hears Angie's voice in her head. Angie is right at the top of the list of people who give her grief about listening to Christmas music so early, and yet, Angie would also be the first one to tell Makenna to crank it if she wants to, because who cares what anyone else thinks?

The school parking lot is filling up, but Makenna pulls her Honda Odyssey into her usual spot. She waves at a couple of moms and turns the ignition off. It's only twenty 'til three, and the girls don't get out of school until three. But she always comes this early, because she's over-protective and can't stand to think of running late and leaving the girls to stand and wait on her. Usually she reads while she waits, and the book she's reading right now—a fluffy, feel-good Christmas romance—is on the passenger seat. But she doesn't feel like reading. Instead, she takes a small notebook from her purse and flips it open to a blank page. Maybe she'll make her Christmas list. Actually, she's kind of late with that. Normally by this time of year, she has half of the girls' presents bought, and she knows if they are even or if she owes one or the other a couple more things.

Aidyn's still pretty easy to buy for. She's all girl, and at six, she's still into Polly Pockets and Barbies and baby dolls. Nothing Santa can't handle there. Ariel's a different story. Santa had brought her a big, ornate dollhouse when she was five, and Makenna's not sure Ariel ever played with it. Ariel thinks it's pretty, and all of her friends have oohed and awed over it through the years. But she'd gone through the doll phase pretty quickly and now prefers sporty things and books and music.

Only so many basketballs and softball gloves you can give a ten-year-old girl. True, she uses all of it, but still, she can only shoot one basketball at a time. Maybe a new bat? But Makenna and Dave had given her a fancy new hot pink bat for her birthday last year. Scratch that. New batting helmet? Nope. Lisa had bought her a helmet one day last summer, just for the heck of it, when she'd had one of her Kid Moments and needed some face time with Ariel.

We can always do clothes. But not from Santa. Makenna raises her eyebrows at the thought. Ariel is on the fence about Santa and has been for at least a year. Makenna figures that when she's with her friends and classmates, Ariel laughs at the idea of little kids believing in magic reindeer and Santa Claus delivering presents to kids all over the world. But at home, she's a little reluctant to admit that. Makenna doesn't blame Ariel. Dave would probably jump all over it, and the minute Aidyn started to question the whole idea, he'd be done with it. No more second Christmas tree. No more presents from Santa. Makenna's no more ready for that than Ariel is.

Games. Ariel still likes to play board games. And video games, especially Xbox games. Makenna jots down a note to check into what Xbox games are popular this year. Maybe the new dance game. Ariel and her friends loved the first one.

Well, so did Makenna and her friends, especially after a couple glasses of wine.

Makenna jumps when someone taps on her window. She looks up to see Karen Craine standing there with a smile plastered to her face. *Joy.* Makenna turns the key and puts the window down a few inches.

"Hey, Makenna." Karen starts out all blustery and out of breath as usual. Makenna smiles politely, but she wants to bang her head on the steering wheel. Karen Craine's not her favorite person and never has been.

"Hi, Karen—"

"Did you get my email? About the first grade class Christmas party?"

"Yeah, I did. It sounds great."

And it did, Makenna had to admit that. Karen had three games planned for them. In the event that they got through those three games, Karen had a Christmas picture for them to color. Two other moms would be bringing cookies and punch for a snack. Makenna kind of felt guilty for not bringing anything, but then she had been in charge of the Halloween class party and she'd brought cupcakes (the janitor hadn't loved that) and those short little cans of soda for the kids.

"I'll be in and out. I have Ariel's party, too."

"Yeah, okay." Karen nods and instead of moving on, she nods down at the notepad in Makenna's lap. "What're you writing?"

Makenna can't wait to tell Angie about this discussion. Angie's not crazy about Karen either.

"Christmas list."

"Yours?"

"No. The girls'."

"Oh. Hey, have you seen that new science lab kit? You know, where kids can—"

The passenger door opens, and Makenna turns to look at Ariel. She'd love to lean over and hug her right now, just for the interruption, but she just winks at her and turns back to Karen.

"Oh. I guess I'd better get up there," Karen says as she looks over her shoulder at the school doors. "First grade might already be out."

"They might," Makenna answers. She says goodbye to Karen and then looks back at Ariel. "Thank you."

"You owe me one." Ariel flips her blonde ponytail off her shoulder and drops her backpack on the floor of the van.

"For what?"

"That rescue. You can pay me in milkshakes or US dollars."

"Rescue was imminent." Makenna shakes her head. "She'd have realized it was time to move on anyway."

"Not before talking your ears off first," Ariel mumbles. "I aced my math test."

"Awesome." Makenna puts her hand out for Ariel's five. "Here comes Aidyn."

She starts to get out of the car but stops when Ariel says something else.

"—hurt in P.E. today."

"You did?"

"No, Aidyn did. They wouldn't let her call you. She fell on her knees."

"Why wouldn't they let her call me?"

"Mrs. Allan said she wasn't hurt that bad, and she didn't need to call you."

Makenna has a very strong dislike for Aidyn's teacher, Mrs. Allan. She thinks the woman is years beyond retirement and much too grouchy for a room full of six-years-olds. Not strict, just plain grouchy.

"How do you know?" Makenna asks Ariel.

"They let me go to the gym for a minute to talk to Aidyn. She's okay, but she was really crying."

Makenna nods and then pushes the door open and slides out. Aidyn, minus her usual bounce and grin, falls against her legs and puts her arms around them.

"Rough day, baby?" Makenna asks.

Aidyn nods against her, but she doesn't say anything.

"I'm sorry you hurt your knee." Makenna picks her up; she's light as a feather. Then again, the child never eats anything but Cheerios.

"My knee's fine," Aidyn answers, but she sounds crabby. "Stupid Jaden Jackson stole my crayon."

"He did? Did you take it back?"

"No. He took gray, and I hate gray so I just called him stupid. If you're gonna steal a crayon, why wouldn't you steal blue or red?"

Makenna laughs as she sets Aidyn back on her feet and pulls her door open for her.

"You're absolutely right," Makenna agrees.

"And then Jaden and Bobby Freeman got in a fight at practice."

"Practice?" Makenna repeats as she climbs back into her own seat and starts the van. She's cold now after being outside for a minute. The temperature must have dropped another five degrees. She looks up at the clouds and wonders if it will snow. Sure looks like it could.

"For the Christmas program, Mo-om," Aidyn says with an angry groan. "Don't you listen to anything?"

Makenna glances at Ariel.

"Tough crowd," Ariel whispers with a shrug.

"I do, Aidyn." Makenna looks into the rearview mirror

and begins to edge out of her spot. "I guess I forgot. Did they get in trouble?"

"We all did," Aidyn snaps. "No recess tomorrow."

"Well, that's fair," Makenna mumbles sarcastically.

Aidyn groans again. "Turn this stupid music off. What happened to the Barney CD?"

"Honey, how about we go home, and you and Ariel can have some cookies and hot chocolate?"

"It's not Christmas yet," Aidyn announces. Makenna glances at her. Aidyn looks the other way, but Makenna can see the frown on her usually sweet face. Her brown eyes are bloodshot and a little glassy. *Great. She's getting sick. Just what we need.*

"Your Barney CD is Christmas music too," Makenna gently reminds her as she pulls out of the parking lot. She's glad, especially on days like today, that the girls go to a small, parochial grade school, and there's no Holy Grail of a System for picking up and dropping off the kids at school.

"Huh?" Aidyn turns to look at Makenna. "That's not what I mean."

"Take a deep breath, Aidyn." Makenna turns the music down again. "What did you mean?"

"It's not Christmas yet. You make cookies and hot chocolate when it's Christmas."

"Oh. Well, I didn't mean sugar cookies. I meant that I could put a few chocolate chip cookies in the oven for you guys. And since it's getting colder, you could have some hot chocolate with them."

When there's no answer, Makenna looks in the rearview mirror again. Aidyn has her head back against the seat, and she looks sleepy.

"Poor baby," she whispers to Ariel. "Want some cookies and hot chocolate, baby?"

"Mm-hmm." Aidyn nods and closes her eyes.

Makenna sighs quietly. Crisis averted. Thank goodness. She hates the days when there are blow-ups on the way home from school. The arguing puts her in a bad mood, which ends up causing a fight between her and Dave.

"Do you have much homework?" she asks Ariel.

"Social Studies," Ariel answers. "And I need to finish reading my book for my report."

Makenna nods. So, maybe they could have a good night, after all. She turns the music up a bit and then glances back at Aidyn, who now looks like an angel deep in sleep.

2

M akenna

"TURN THAT OFF!" ANGIE EDWARDS LUNGES FOR THE remote, but Makenna dodges her.

She holds the remote behind her back and shakes her finger at Angie. Theirs is a thirty-year-old friendship. Easy, like comfortable, worn jeans. Maybe each year they share this scene with only slight variations. Makenna wonders where the magic of the season has gone, why she feels like she moves by rote memorization and what would happen if she changed the script without telling anyone else.

Still laughing, Makenna narrows her eyes at Angie. "Do not spill that wine on my carpet."

"I'm not on the carpet," Angie answers and reaches again for the remote control. "Turn the music off."

"You're pretty damned close, and cab sav isn't going to look good on ivory-colored carpet."

"Not to mention that'd be alcohol abuse," Brian, Angie's husband, says as he squeezes between them to help himself to a cracker and a slice of summer sausage.

"This is new music," Makenna tells Angie. True enough. Her Christmas playlist grows exponentially year after year.

"How can you tell?" Angie takes a drink of her wine. "Seriously, Ken, how can you listen to that and tell that it's new?"

"I just got it last weekend."

Angie laughs and rolls her eyes.

"You really want me to turn it off?" Makenna drapes her arm over Angie's shoulders.

"No, because then Aidyn will want you to put in Barney," Piper says with a shudder.

Angie laughs at her daughter and shakes her head. "You used to love Barney."

"Yeah, when I was three," Piper answers. "Just. Eew. Isn't there something new out there yet? Kids shouldn't be listening to a big purple dinosaur—"

"Who's a big purple dinosaur?" Aidyn yanks on Piper's hand and looks up at her.

Makenna cringes, because she doesn't want to listen to Barney, either, but she has to laugh.

"Barney," Piper tells her. Recently fifteen, Piper seems to have grown up overnight. Makenna feels a pang of sadness as she watches Piper talk to Aidyn. Seems like just yesterday that Piper was their only baby, when the four of them—well, seven, including the guys—used to play pass the baby and spoil her.

"What's wrong with Barney?" Aidyn asks calmly as she climbs up on a barstool at Makenna's kitchen bar.

"Yeah, Piper. What's wrong with Barney?" Makenna asks her.

Piper shoots Makenna a look that tells her she's clearly behind the times.

"Right." Makenna nods and pours herself more wine. She sees Angie watching her and trying to tamp down her laughter.

"I like Barney," Aidyn tells Piper. She reaches for a cookie, and Makenna lets her. She hasn't eaten much today, and Makenna knows she'll eat a bite of this cookie and then throw it away. Aidyn's doctor says she's fine if she eats when she's hungry. She's small for her age, but she did grow a bit taller and put on a couple of pounds through the summer.

Makenna still worries.

"Yeah, but don't you like anybody else?" Piper turns sideways on her own barstool so she can talk directly to Aidyn. "Like *The Backyardigans* or *Dora* or something?"

"*Dora's* for babies."

Piper snorts and glances at Makenna and Angie. They wait quietly to see what Piper will say.

"Really? You don't like *Dora the Explorer*? Because I do. I like Swiper."

Aidyn shakes her head. "Nope. I like *iCarly*."

"What?" Piper draws back, surprised by Aidyn's answer. "*iCarly*? That show's too old for you!"

"I like Freddy," Aidyn says as she takes a bite of the cookie and then very carefully places it on a napkin. If only Ariel were as tidy as Aidyn.

"I watched stuff like Barney when I was your age," Piper announces. She takes a big drink of her ice water.

"You just said dinosaurs are eeww," Aidyn says as Angie laughs and shakes her head.

"Barney's okay for a dinosaur," Angie interrupts the conversation. "And Piper, hate to tell you, but you watched stuff like *Even Stevens* and *Lizzie McGuire*."

"Mom, you're not helping," Piper mumbles without turning to look at Angie.

"Where'd you say Lisa is?" Angie asks and turns back to Makenna.

"Grading papers," Makenna answers with a shrug. It is the Saturday before Thanksgiving, and as she has done every year for the past ten, Makenna has invited them over for their Friends Thanksgiving. It's like Makenna's family Thanksgiving in every way, except they aren't related by blood, and Makenna does the turkey. When she and Dave and the girls go to her mom's for dinner, her mom fixes the turkey.

"My ass," Angie says into her wine glass. Makenna grins but keeps her back to Angie. She checks the potatoes and decides they are done boiling. "She's so sleeping with that guy."

That gets Makenna's attention. She turns quickly to look at Angie.

"What guy?"

"That Jack guy. Jack Holloman or whatever his name is."

"The one who's subbing right now? For that other teacher she knows?"

"The one and only." Angie puts her wineglass down

and shoves the sleeves of her sweater up. "Here. Let me do the noodles while you whip the potatoes."

"You always do the noodles," Makenna argues.

"So why change a good thing?"

"Why do you say she's sleeping with him?"

"Ken. They've been seeing each other for a few weeks now. And c'mon. Really? Working? On a Saturday night?"

"She said she had some papers to grade and then she'd be over."

"She's not grading papers."

"Why couldn't she just bring him here? As her date?"

Angie slips oven mitts on her hands and lifts the pot of noodles from the burner.

"You'd have to ask her that."

"Where's Lisa?" Jamie Maczum's voice suddenly intrudes on their conversation. Makenna relaxes against him as he puts his arm around her shoulders. She and Angie bump heads when he pulls Angie into his other arm. "She's never been this late."

"Grading papers," Makenna tells him and shoots Angie a warning look. They both want Lisa to find the right guy. More than that, they want Lisa to find love, true love—the kind that will give her a happy marriage and children.

But both of them know that as long as Jamie Maczum wears a wedding band on his finger, Lisa won't find true love or a happy marriage. They've often talked about it, and both of them wonder how Jamie can be so blind.

Lisa Fairchild has been in love with him and denying being in love with him for the past twenty years. Though a happily married father of two, Jamie's as in love with Lisa as he is with his wife.

Makenna dreads the moment he figures it out, but not as much as she dreads the day his wife realizes it.

———

WHEN DINNER IS FINISHED, THE GUYS CRASH IN THE LIVING room in front of the TV. The after dinner clean up isn't one of Makenna's favorite holiday traditions. In fact, she'd rather go sink into the couch and stare at the TV.

The kids are downstairs. She can hear music and giggling, so she assumes they are playing the dance game on the Wii. She wonders if Piper is playing. It's inevitable that Piper grows up and grows away from all of them, but she hates that it's happening. In years past, Piper would have been up to her neck in cookie dough or been front and center while saying the prayer they always say before meals. Today, Piper spent a big chunk of time curled up on the sectional in the basement reading a book. Probably something about vampires, though Makenna didn't look that closely.

She doesn't blame her. It's hard for teenagers to fit in with the little kids. Sure, it'd get boring for Piper to play Chutes and Ladders or Uno, when she's playing with the likes of Aidyn. It's just as hard for Piper to fit in with the women in the kitchen. She can hang for so long, but she either gets bored with the discussions about jobs or illness or bills to be paid, or she is embarrassed by something slightly personal or blatantly raunchy, and she high-tails it out of the kitchen.

Makenna hears Piper's voice from downstairs. She's cheering Ariel on. Good. Ariel worships the ground Piper walks on. Makenna hopes Piper takes a turn and doesn't just sit and watch. She won't have to wonder long when everyone leaves. Ariel will tell her.

"Someone say something funny." Lisa's voice cuts through the chatter. Makenna stills her hands in the dishwater and looks at Lisa like she suddenly has a third eyeball. Lisa's hands, wrapped in a dishtowel, hold a serving bowl. She grins at Makenna and bats her eyelashes. Jamie's wife, Brooke, and Angie, both putting away dry dishes and pots and pans, don't pay attention to them. They are hip-deep in their own conversation.

"What?"

"You had that really serious, pensive look going." Lisa shrugs. "You're thinking too much. This is our holiday."

Makenna smiles, but she can't shake the way thinking about Piper growing up makes her sad. If Piper's growing up, the kids are *all* growing up. And if the kids are growing up, she and her friends are all growing old.

"Stop it." Lisa reaches out and touches Makenna's arm. "Happy thoughts. You know the rules."

She does know the rules. Of the four of them, Makenna is the one most susceptible to the Christmas blues. Her friends forbid her to feel sad or wistful on their days of celebration, and this is one of their biggest days.

"Why don't you share some happy thoughts with me?" Makenna suggests. Lisa ducks her head immediately.

"What?"

"Where were you tonight?"

"Grading—"

"Lisa." Makenna throws her hip gently against Lisa's.

"If you know, why are you asking?"

"I don't really know. I don't know much at all." Makenna glances around to see how they are coming with cleaning. She spots three pans on the stove, but before she can move, Angie steps over and grabs them one at a time, all without interrupting her conversation with Brooke. "You haven't told us much at all."

Lisa considers this for a moment.

"Probably against the rules to get into this conversation tonight," she finally answers. Makenna raises her eyebrows. That means there's definitely something going on, and it must not be sweet and romantic or hot and sexy. Lisa has something on her mind.

"Why didn't you bring him with you?"

"Yeah." Jamie's voice is suddenly right behind them. "Why didn't you bring him? Isn't it about time I meet him?"

Makenna watches the emotions play over Lisa's face. If Makenna gets frustrated with Jamie always being involved in Lisa's relationships, how must Lisa feel? Makenna looks away and concentrates on scrubbing the roaster pan in the sink. She doesn't want to see the look of defeat on Lisa's face.

In fact, she wants to turn around and look at Jamie and ask him if it isn't about time he leave Lisa alone and let her be free to fall for someone else.

Which would definitely throw a wrench into the evening and every other evening they might ever plan together as a group.

"Grab me a beer, Maczum!" Brian yells from the living room. Jamie winks at them and then moves away to grab a couple of beers from the cooler in the mudroom that Dave always stocks for their get-togethers. The red cooler is full of soda and juice drinks for the kids, and the blue cooler is always full of bottled beer.

"Sorry," she says quietly to Lisa.

Lisa shrugs and sighs. "For the record, I was grading papers earlier. I got caught up reading the kids' Thanksgiving poems. Some of them were really good."

"I think this is it," Angie announces as she sets the meat serving platter on the counter by the sink. "Want me to finish them up?"

"Nope. I got it."

"Playing Uno or Spoons?" Brooke asks as she leans against the counter.

"I almost had to have stitches last year when we played Spoons!" Angie laughs.

"It was a scratch." Makenna gives Angie a stern look. "You lived."

"Okay, but you can't wear your rings."

"Whatever. Your ring's twice as big as mine."

"Diamond envy." Angie is joking, but her words grate on Makenna's nerves. She wonders what they do to Lisa. She is the only one of them who has never been married or engaged. She's always been the first to run when she's been involved with anyone.

"Piper will want to play," she says as she pulls the sink stopper out to drain the water.

"Yeah, but it sounds like she's having fun downstairs with the kids." Angie pours herself more wine. The bottle is empty. Brooke turns to eye the wine rack in the corner of the kitchen. Makenna feels a pang inside, knowing that Brooke is so comfortable in her home that she will help herself to something she wants or needs.

What happens when three people you love are on a collision course? And the crash is going to cause major fall-out and your own home is going to be part of the site?

3

M akenna

SHE SCREENS HER CALLS WHEN SHE'S WORKING, AND MOST often, she ignores them. But the doorbell doesn't ring that often, and she finds it harder to just ignore the fact that someone is standing on the front porch. She sighs and blows her dirty blond bangs off her forehead.

Surprised to find that it's almost noon, she leaves her office to answer the door. She's even more surprised to find Brooke on her porch.

"Hey!" Makenna swallows the rush of confusion and reaches out to Brooke. She pulls her inside and quickly closes the door. The temperature has dropped twenty degrees since yesterday. It most definitely feels like the holidays now.

Though she and Brooke are friends, it's not often that

Brooke shows up, by herself, at her house. In fact, Makenna can probably count those instances on one finger. Today.

"Man, it's cold out there," Brooke groans as she unbuttons her coat. Makenna wonders if she plans to stay long. Not that she has that much left to do for the CordonINC newsletter she's been working on. It's more that she's not sure what to do with Brooke Maczum in her house. *Just Brooke*. And no Jamie or Lisa or Angie.

"I know. Aidyn's praying for snow," Makenna says with a laugh. "I'm not ready for that."

"Eh. Me neither." Brooke shakes her long blond hair out. "Do you have a minute?"

"Yeah." Makenna reaches for Brooke's coat. "What's up?"

"I brought that recipe for pumpkin bread. You can do it for your family Thanksgiving."

"Oh!" Makenna nods and takes it when Brooke fishes it out of her purse. It's written in perfect hand on a small index card. At the top, preprinted blue letters say *From Brooke's Kitchen*. For just a minute, Makenna wishes it said *From Lisa's Kitchen*. But then she's not so sure how that would work. Lisa's never cooked anything more than macaroni and cheese and green bean casserole, which is what she brings to their get-togethers. No matter what the occasion.

Makenna gives herself a mental shake. Lisa isn't obsessing over this stuff, so why is she? It's not like it's her business anyway. She looks again at Brooke, takes a moment while Brooke steps out of her shoes to really study her. She could have emailed the recipe. Makenna doubts that she drove it over just so it would be on that cute little index card with Brooke's name on it. Something's up.

Which makes Makenna nervous.

"Want some coffee?" she asks when Brooke stands up straight and looks at her again.

"Sure," Brooke agrees. Makenna sees her glance into the office as they walk by. "You're working. I should've called."

"No, it's okay." Makenna takes a coffee mug from the cabinet and pours Brooke a cup.

"Is yours in the office?" Brooke asks. Makenna sets out the cream and sugar.

"Yeah, I'll get it."

Okay, so it's kind of nice to have a visitor. She's still a bit afraid of whatever is on Brooke's mind, but she does like her, and it's always nice to kick back with a cup of coffee and a friend and some conversation.

She does a quick save on the newsletter she'd been working on, grabs her nearly empty mug, and heads back out to the kitchen. Brooke sits at the bar, already sipping her coffee.

"No Christmas music?"

Makenna laughs as she pours herself more coffee. "Contrary to Angie's belief, I don't listen to it twenty-four seven. I'd go as nuts as the next person."

"I don't take you for a Frank Sinatra kind of girl."

Makenna stirs cream into her coffee and avoids Brooke's eyes. Frank Sinatra's voice surrounds them and tells them about "Sweet Lorraine."

"Well, I like it because it reminds me of Christmas music."

If Brooke were Angie, she'd laugh. She'd laugh her butt

off and then say something about how she's right, and Makenna listens to Christmas music twenty-four seven. If she were Lisa, she'd shrug and move the conversation on. But Brooke doesn't do either.

She nods.

"I know what you mean."

Their gaze holds, and Makenna suddenly feels the true distance between them. Lisa and Jamie separate them, as they always have, no matter how each of them tries to pretend it isn't so. Makenna's curious as to whether or not Brooke does know what she means, because sometimes she thinks no one really gets her. But she straddles the moment of asking or not, knowing that Brooke has something on her mind, and it could very well be Jamie and Lisa.

Makenna and Angie have been best friends since third grade. Thirty-some years of sharing secrets and clothes and books and music. Thirty-some years of finishing each other's sentences and nursing each other's broken hearts with just a look or a hug. Thirty-some years of that hard, shooting soda out of your nose kind of laughter.

Lisa didn't enter the picture until junior high. With coal black hair and big brown eyes, she'd rounded out their group well. Angie has red hair, though now she tends to play with the color on a regular basis, and Makenna used to have really blond hair. Age has brought a deeper color that Makenna thinks of as dishwater blond, and Angie says is a honey-wheat blond. Maybe if she were a crayon that would work for her.

Lisa had never posed a threat to their friendship. Maybe because at the same time she met them, she met Jamie Maczum. Lisa's dad had moved her to their school after a tough divorce and losing his job. He'd moved from a pretty nice house in an upper scale neighborhood to a pretty small place in a pretty average neighborhood. Lisa had grown as close to Jamie as fast as she'd grown close to Makenna and Angie.

To this day, Lisa swears there's nothing more than friendship between her and Jamie.

Maybe they've never slept together, but Makenna knows there's a hell of a lot more to Lisa and Jamie than a simple friendship.

"It's that big band kind of sound," Brooke says now. Makenna breaks the eye contact and stares down into her coffee. "It's kind of a happy sound. A little old-fashioned."

Makenna nods in spite of herself. "Kind of like innocence put to music."

Brooke tucks a lock of hair behind her ear. "Exactly. Wonder what Sinatra would think of rap?"

Makenna raises her eyebrows. "I'd say he's probably turning over in his grave with the way things have changed," she says with a grin, "but then I'd sound like my mom."

Brooke laughs.

"I applied for a job today," she says suddenly.

"What? You did?" Makenna slides sideways onto a barstool. She pulls one socked foot up under her thigh. She and Angie have spent many mornings parked in these same spots talking about everything from music to the neighbors to pregnancies. It feels both good and odd to sit here with Brooke this way.

Brooke sighs. "I just...the kids are getting older. I'm kind of going nuts sitting around the house all the time."

Makenna understands that, but then again, she doesn't

totally get it. True, Aidyn is still very young, and Makenna loves being home for her every day. But even if Aidyn were older, Makenna would still choose to work from home. For one thing, her small desktop publishing business is very much what she enjoys doing. But it's more than that. She's certainly not agoraphobic, and she's not antisocial, but she loves her alone time and guards it viciously.

Her friends, including Brooke, know that.

"I talked to Daniel and Jared about it a few days ago."

Makenna cocks her head and waits for Brooke to say more.

"They couldn't care less," she continues, "as long as someone is doing their laundry and putting food on the table for them. I don't think they notice I'm even around anymore."

Makenna wants to argue, but she can't. Daniel will be thirteen in December, and Jared is eleven, in the same grade as Angie's son, Zach. Both of them are good kids, but they aren't the clingy type. Daniel is well on his way to becoming a basketball star, and Jared is as good or better at soccer. Now that they're older, they spend more time with Jamie than with Brooke.

She has no plans to go back to work anywhere, but Makenna understands the hurt, the loneliness it brings when you realize you aren't really needed anymore. Thank goodness, she and Ariel are pretty close, but Ariel doesn't really *need* her anymore. Not like she used to.

"Where did you apply?" Makenna asks again.

"I interviewed this morning," Brooke answers, and Makenna wonders why she is avoiding the question. Makenna notices now that Brooke is wearing dark slacks and a colorful blouse. Not the usual attire of jeans and sweatshirts, the stay-at-home mom attire Makenna prefers.

"Where?" Makenna pushes. Brooke is a nurse by education and experience. She'd worked in the ob-gyn department at the clinic for a few years before she'd quit to stay at home with her boys. Makenna wonders where she could get a job and still be home after school to fix dinner and keep the home fires burning.

"There's an opening for a school nurse," Brooke answers finally.

"Oh." Makenna doesn't know if she actually said the word or if she's just thinking it. Brooke doesn't have to say it. She'd interviewed at the junior high, where Jamie is a math teacher and the basketball coach and where he's been eyeballing the assistant principal's position since the older man had mentioned retirement sometime last year.

Where Lisa teaches eighth grade English.

Where maybe Brooke, if she got the job, might have to see looks pass between Lisa and her husband. Where maybe neither Lisa nor Jamie would want her to work, because maybe school is the one place where they don't have to hide how they feel about each other.

That's ridiculous, Makenna.

She takes a drink, and the coffee's too hot. It burns her tongue.

Lisa and Jamie are not having an affair, and even if they are, they sure aren't feeling each other up and professing undying love in the halls of the junior high building.

"That's good, Brooke," Makenna says, and she's surprised that her voice sounds normal. "That'd give you great hours so you could still get home and get the boys dinner and get them to their practices and stuff."

"Yeah." Brooke's mouth turns down at one corner, and she frowns. "I guess."

"Having second thoughts?"

"Kind of."

"Why? What's going on?"

She's not sure she wants to know. She's not sure she should have asked. But, the words are out now, and she can't take them back. Even though Brooke is her friend, if push comes to shove, Makenna's loyalty is to Lisa. Then again, they're adults and thinking about loyalty and listening to a friend seems pretty immature.

Except there's no real problem with breaking up marriages in junior high.

"I feel like..." Brooke takes a shaky breath.

Makenna wishes Angie were here. This isn't something she wants to deal with alone.

"Like I'm intruding."

Makenna frowns, but before she can say anything, Brooke starts talking again.

"Like being at work is the one place where they can still have that special bond. The one place where maybe I don't exist to them, and now here I am trying to step in on what they have."

"What're you talking about?"

"Makenna," Brooke groans. "C'mon. You know I'm talking about Jamie and Lisa."

"You think they have something going on at school?"

"No, no." Brooke shakes her head. "No, I don't think they have something going on. That's just it. I think so many people see them and think they do, and they don't. I just think that Jamie's family…that *I've*…really changed their friendship. I feel guilty that I just did something that might wreck the one place where they can be friends without having to talk around me."

Makenna frowns. She watches her fingers nudge at her coffee cup. There's a chip in her French manicure. Coffee sloshes over the side of her cup. It's still hot. She sticks her finger in her mouth and looks up at Brooke.

"I don't know what to say to that."

"Don't insult me by pretending you don't know what I'm saying."

"Oh, I'm not," Makenna answers quickly. "I just have no idea how to respond."

"You think I'm wrong?"

"To interview for a job there? No." Makenna stands up and takes her coffee cup to the sink. Dumping it is a good excuse to keep her back to Brooke. She no longer wishes Angie were here to talk for her. She wishes Angie were here to sensor what she might end up saying.

Love Lisa or not, Makenna believes in marriage, most especially the part where two people say *till death do us part.*

"Do you think I overstepped?"

"No." Makenna turns back to Brooke. She shakes her head and folds her arms over her chest. "No, I don't."

"But?"

"But nothing." Makenna sighs. "I don't think a wife or husband should ever come second to friendship. I don't think you should have to worry about coming between them."

Brooke studies Makenna with narrowed eyes. "Really?"

"Yeah."

"What if it weren't Jamie and Lisa?"

"What do you mean?"

"What if it was just Jamie on this job? And I was hired on, and suddenly Jamie feels different, and it's because I'm there. I'm his wife, and I've just taken away a space where he's just Jamie."

Makenna clears her throat and starts to answer her. She wants to tell Brooke that it shouldn't matter. Brooke is important, and Jamie should be comfortable with this kind of situation. But she can't. Because when Brooke phrases it this way, she does think Brooke has overstepped. Maybe everyone does need his or her own space to be free of being married. Not free of the vows, but free to let other things become more important and more fun for a few hours each day.

"I overstepped."

"How much would you even be working around either of them?" Makenna avoids Brooke's comment.

"That's not the point. You know how a work environment is. People talk. I don't even mean rumors. People talk, and I would be hearing stuff about Jamie. About Lisa. And they would know things about me." Brooke groans and runs her fingers through her hair. "I shouldn't have done it. I wasn't thinking."

"Can you pass on the job if they offer it?"

Brooke nods.

"Are you okay with that? It sounds like you're really wanting out of the house."

"I can look for something else." She looks up at Makenna with a sad smile. "I just heard about the position opening, and I jumped the gun. Didn't think."

Makenna wonders how she would feel if she were in Brooke's shoes. What would it be like if Dave's best friend was a woman? A gorgeous, single woman. Could she allow a close relationship between them the way Brooke has?

"Lisa's doing Thanksgiving with Jack," Brooke announces suddenly.

"Really? She hasn't been seeing him that long, has she?"

Brooke cocks her head a bit and stares at Makenna silently. "Since last May."

"What?"

How has Lisa been seeing someone for six months when Makenna didn't even know? She'd known they'd gone out a few times, but Makenna had no idea there was anything serious going on between them.

And why does Brooke know? Surely Lisa hasn't discussed Jack with Jamie. She used to talk to Jamie about every guy she dated. But she got tired of Jamie being over-protective, and she stopped introducing him to most guys she went out with.

"Well, they haven't been serious for that long. But it's been awhile."

"I didn't know that."

"His sister does Thanksgiving dinner. She lives in Champagne."

Makenna turns away and hopes that Brooke doesn't see the way her words sting. Once upon a time, Lisa had told her and Angie everything. She wonders when that changed.

"Sounds like fun." She laughs softly. "I hope she doesn't have to take anything."

Brooke grins. "I told her to take a bottle of wine."

"You're gonna have to teach her how to cook when she gets married."

Brooke nods, and she's still laughing as she makes her way back down the front hall to the door. Neither of them comments on the unspoken words. They ignore the way they echo around the house.

If she gets married.

Because who would Lisa marry, if Jamie is happily married to Brooke?

4

L isa

THE TEMPERATURE HAS DROPPED AGAIN, AND IT'S BEEN snowing for the better part of an hour. The tiny little flakes sparkle in the streetlights as they come down, and Lisa finds herself mesmerized by them. She stomps her feet on the ground to warm up. She doesn't have to be standing outside to enjoy looking at the snow, but she does have to be outside to be by Jack at the moment.

He looks up at her after he slides the gas pump into his SUV. Chalk it up to this ridiculous teenager-in-love feeling, but Lisa thinks his green eyes are sparkling.

"You could have waited in the truck," he tells her, but he's smiling, and she knows he's glad she's standing outside by him while he pumps gas. It's just after five, but already darkness is falling, and the cold folds itself over her shoulders like a cloak. At the very least, she could have put her coat on when she got out.

She shrugs and looks around. The city—Quincy is not a metropolis, but with a population upward of forty-thousand it's not a hole in the wall either—is lit up with the normal nighttime marquees and streetlights. But Lisa feels it is something more.

"You want some coffee?" she asks. It's a long drive to Champagne, and because they both worked all day, they are starting late. Maybe Jack needs coffee to stay awake while he's driving. Lisa knows she doesn't need coffee. She's wound so tightly at the moment that Jack could touch her and feel a low hum of vibration inside her.

But she wants coffee just the same. Not just coffee. Something frilly and fun with a holiday name. Something pepperminty or egg-noggy. She glances at the convenience store and raises her eyebrows. Okay, so she's not going to find anything too fancy here, but she's sure she'll find something fun.

"How about we hit Billy's Beans on the way out Broadway?" Jack suggests, and Lisa wonders yet again if he can read her mind.

"Really?" She grins. "You'd get me something even if we are running late?"

Jack steps toward her and leans in to press his lips to the corner of her eye. "First of all, we're not running late. It's you and me, and we've got all night. Second, I think you want something frilly and holidayish, don't you? You don't want coffee. You want atmosphere. To go."

"How do you know me so well?" she mumbles, but her words are lost in the kiss. Probably she should be mindful of where she is. Probably she shouldn't be French-kissing

—and God yes, this man kisses good enough that she can only think in terms of French-kissing—right out in public. Any number of students or parents or faculty members could drive by or pull into this gas station and see the eighth grade English teacher engaged in a seriously intense public display of affection.

But she doesn't care. Not at the moment. True, it's Thanksgiving vacation, not Christmas. But she feels particularly light-hearted right now. Happy. Fear prevents her from admitting that to anyone but herself, but right at this moment, she's happy.

"I'd like that," she says as she finally pulls away from Jack. Not that she wants to, but she does have to breathe. Kissing like this, outside in the cold, might chap their lips. Then kissing Jack later might hurt, and she plans to kiss Jack later.

"Jingle Bells" plays from her hip pocket. Jack grins and nods at her.

"Take it in the car. No sense in standing out here freezing."

She's not that cold now. Not with her blood racing after that kiss. But she goes back to the passenger door and climbs in.

"Can wet lips get frostbite?" she asks instead of saying hello, because she knows from her caller ID that it's Angie.

"I'm just not even going to answer that, and I'm gonna forget the question completely."

"Okay," Lisa says and fiddles with her earring. "What's up?"

"Makenna says you're doing Thanksgiving with Jack's family."

"Yeah." Lisa knows she doesn't have to explain herself to Angie, and yet she feels a tiny bit bad about not telling her or Makenna herself.

"Well. Okay." Angie seems a bit lost for words. And the tiny bit of bad grows into a bit of a stomachache. "In Champagne? Have you left yet?"

"Jack's pumping gas right now. Then we're gonna hit Billy's and head out."

"Oh." Angie recovers herself much quicker than Makenna would have. "Okay. Well, have fun, okay? Just enjoy the hell out of it. And eat pie. You never eat enough pie."

Lisa laughs, and she does feel better. But she still feels a little guilty for not sitting down and talking to Angie and Makenna about Jack. What would they say if they knew she and Brooke had sat and talked until two in the morning a couple of weeks ago?

"I promise. But I'm pretty sure I won't find any apple pie as good as yours."

"Please. You peel apples and slice them and toss on some cinnamon—"

"Ang, you're a baking goddess," Lisa tells her. "Don't deny it."

"Have fun."

"You're not mad, are you?" Lisa says softly. For the past twenty years, she, Angie, Makenna, and Jamie have spent the holidays together. She can count on one hand the number of times she hasn't been with her best friends.

"No!" Angie says quickly. Too quickly? "Of course not! We'll miss you, but it's cool. Just have fun."

"Thanks, Ang."

"Call me when you get back. Okay?"

"I will."

Lisa taps her phone to end the call and drops it in the console as Jack yanks the driver's door open and gets in.

"One of the crew, I assume."

"Who else calls me?" she asks with a smile. Of course, her best friends are going to want to know what she's doing for Thanksgiving and to wish her safe travels and a fun trip. But when she hears her own words, she can't help but feel a little sad. *Who else would call her? Her boss? Jack?*

As much as she loves her friends, sometimes she wishes there were more to her life. Sometimes envy nearly rips her apart when she's with her best friends and their families. She wants what they have. Of course, she does. Of course, she wants marriage. Someone to love her madly, the way Dave and Brian love Makenna and Angie. The way Jamie loves Brooke.

Of course, she wants babies. She wants a baby girl to dress in pink and ribbons and bows or a baby boy who might have his daddy's eyes. Of course, she wants it all.

Sometimes it kills her to watch her friends, the people she loves most in the world, hold everything in the palms of their hands and not realize how precious their lives are. But sometimes it infuriates her to know that Makenna and Angie believe the reason she's not married is because Jamie already is. What's worse is wondering if they're right.

Irritated with Angie for calling and taking the shine off her weekend (irrational, she knows) and irritated with herself for allowing it, she forces the doubts from her mind and turns to Jack. He slows to turn into the coffee shop.

"It was Angie. Someone told her we were going to Champagne for Thanksgiving."

"You didn't?" he asks quickly.

"I haven't talked to her for a few days," Lisa hedges. True, she hasn't. But she could have. She could have called Angie or Makenna to discuss her plans, but she didn't.

"You haven't told them about us. Have you?"

"I have," she answers truthfully. She has told them she's been seeing Jack, but she hasn't gone into much detail. For one thing, seems like every time she wants to talk about Jack, Jamie is around.

"Whatcha want?" he asks as he eases into the drive-thru.

"Mmm." She leans toward him so she can see the menu board. He reaches toward her and slides his hand up her side. "Mm-hmm. I want a whole lot of that, but probably not here."

He chuckles and pushes himself back out of her way so she can see the menu clearly.

"Peppermint Mocha," she says and smacks a kiss on his lips before she sits back again.

"Anything to eat?"

"No, thanks," she answers. "I ate some leftover pizza while I was packing."

"You sure? No muffin or cookie or anything?"

"No."

She watches the snow fall as he orders and wishes she'd have brought her iPod. Jack might be the type of guy to swing in and buy her a Peppermint Mocha, but she's pretty sure she's not going to find a Christmas playlist on his iPod.

Oh well. She leans her head back and closes her eyes.

This will be the first Thanksgiving she's spent with a man, other than her married best friend and her other friend's husbands, since she was nineteen.

Maybe this time will be the beginning of something, rather than the end.

5

A ngie

ANGIE, HER HUNGER SATED WITH MORE TURKEY AND noodles and dressing than she'd ever need, sits back in her chair and surreptitiously glances around her aunt's dining room table. She'd like to freeze the moment on film: Uncle Tom pouring more wine for himself and Uncle Bob both, Piper's plate piled with turkey and gravy, Aunt Nora listening to Aunt Janet telling a story, and the younger boys at the other end of the table playing with their food. Brian and her cousin's husband, Eric, are talking about football, while her cousins are arguing college basketball. It's possibly the same scene every year, but every year Angie sees it for the first time. She considers going upstairs for her camera, but she's so tired. Besides, the person behind the camera may be important, the one to preserve the memories, but watching life unfold through a camera lens is so much less than being a part of the moments as they occur.

Whatever, Ang, she thinks. She's being lazy. She probably just gained a good five pounds, if not ten. She loves Aunt Janet's dressing, and she loves Aunt Nora's noodles. And there's still dessert. Though there are only fifteen people at their dinner table, there is always enough food and dessert to feed an army. It's never wasted, though. They all eat leftovers. Brian and Zach like leftover turkey sandwiches with mayonnaise better than turkey with gravy. And Piper will eat noodles the rest of the week. And a piece or two of apple pie. Of course, then she'll gripe until Christmas about how fat she is, only to do it all over again at Christmas dinner and the days following.

She guesses that's what the New Year is for. Making resolutions. Turning over a new leaf.

Even though it's a family day, Angie can't help but think about Lisa. She wonders how things are going at Jack's sister's house, and she wonders about Jack himself. She and Makenna have met him, but they haven't really spent much time around him so they don't know him well.

They've always spent the weekends before and after Thanksgiving together. Lisa has always joined one of them for Thanksgiving dinner, except the year when she went to Colorado with that cowboy wannabe. Lisa was nineteen, and the cowboy was twenty-seven. Angie had figured it was a mistake from the moment Lisa shared her plans. Lisa had figured it out the second the cowboy's truck hit the highway. He hadn't wanted a date to take home to his family. He'd wanted some playtime, away from his wife and son. A wife and son Lisa hadn't even known about.

Lisa's dad had moved to Florida after she graduated from high school. She'd never felt particularly close to him, so she hadn't wanted to move. Instead, she'd let her friends—Makenna, Angie and Jamie—adopt her into their families. The only other times they had deviated from those unspoken plans were the years when Lisa had strep throat, once over Thanksgiving and once over Christmas.

Angie gives herself a mental shake. Lisa's an adult, and she has the right to spend her holidays as she wants. Actually, Angie's kind of excited for her. But she's worried, too. Jack appears to be a nice guy, what Angie knows of him anyway. But there'd never been a man to make Lisa fall out of love with Jamie.

This isn't the time to worry about Lisa, so Angie decides to get her camera. Maybe she's kidding herself, but going upstairs to get the camera from her purse is exercise, right? After the meal she's just eaten and the dessert she'll be eating in five minutes, any little bit of exercise helps.

Piper glances at her as she ducks into the doorway to the steps. Piper grins and licks gravy from her fingers, and for just a moment, Angie is reminded of Piper as a little girl. When she would sit on her knees and lean into the table, her food, and any conversation she could hear. Blond hair, which she'd apparently gotten from someone in Brian's side of the family, swinging over her shoulders and sometimes getting in her gravy. Blue eyes, also from Brian's family, twinkling and the curve of her lips in a big grin. Piper is now model material with her prominent cheekbones and long, graceful neck. Angie loves her, and she's very proud of the young woman who continues to emerge from that little girl she used to be.

But she misses the little girl. Every day, she misses the little girl Piper used to be. But even more so on holidays, when Piper regresses for the day to that happy, high-spirited child. It doesn't seem right that Piper is talking about college applications and scholarships. In fact, it nearly kills Angie to think about it. So, she doesn't. When Piper broaches the subject, Angie covers her ears and sings. One of these days, she'll have to stop. It's time to take Piper seriously, no matter how much it hurts her to do so.

"What're you doing?" Aunt Nora follows her upstairs. She carries the nearly empty turkey platter in one hand and a stack of plates in the other. Angie wants to kick herself for not carrying something up. Aunt Nora and Aunt Janet don't need to do all the work.

"Getting my camera," Angie answers her. "I'm sorry. I should've carried that stuff for you."

"Nah." Aunt Nora shakes her head. "I still think it's the guys' turn for KP duty."

"Hasn't it been their turn for the last twenty years?"

"Twenty, heck. How about forty?"

Angie grins. She finds her purse in the hall closet and digs her camera out. In the kitchen again, Aunt Nora is piling more turkey on the meat platter. Angie feels a pang as she thinks of her mom, gone two years now. Aunt Nora is her mom's older sister, and Aunt Janet is the youngest. Aunt Janet looks so much like her mom that sometimes Angie can't stand it. But Aunt Nora's voice is so much like her mom's that when she has her back turned and hears Aunt Nora talking, she sometimes forgets that her mom is gone, and she turns to answer, only to see Nora and to have that horrible pain take her breath away all over again.

Determined not to break down this year as she has in the two that have gone by since her mom passed away, Angie clears her throat.

"What can I do?" she asks, surprised that her voice isn't abnormally high and tight with tears.

"Take this downstairs for me?" Aunt Nora reaches for a plate of cookies and brownies. The kids don't eat pie, which blows Angie away because who doesn't love pie, so Aunt Nora always has dozens of cookies and brownies ready for them.

"Sure." She takes the plate as Aunt Nora hands it to her. Their eyes meet, and dammit all, Angie feels the tears well.

"You okay?"

Angie nods quickly and turns to hurry down the stairs. The scene is the same, except now it's blurred from the tears she refuses to cry. She sets the heaping plate of cookies on the table and barely gets her hand out of the way before the boys converge on it. Eyes still burning, she checks her pockets for a tissue and finds none.

Instead, she blinks a few times to clear her eyes. But Piper sees her and knows instantly what she is thinking. Feeling. Probably, Angie would not have survived losing her mom if it weren't for Piper. Brian had been there, yes, and Zach, and even Angie's dad. But somehow knowing that Piper was there, in those hard, teenage years and needing Angie gave her the strength to go on.

She's afraid that Piper will say something now. Something that her dad might hear and then maybe the whole atmosphere at the table will change. Angie doesn't want that. There's a time to remember her mom. There is always a time to remember her mom when her family is gathered. But not yet.

Not yet.

She takes a deep breath and looks at Piper bravely. Piper offers her a smile. That's all she needs to find her way back to this moment, not the one that has defined her for the past two years.

Without calling attention to anyone at the table, because Angie likes candid shots as much or more than those that are posed, she begins snapping pictures. Uncle Tom with his wine glass in hand and a smile on his face. Aunt Janet stealing a cookie from Zach's plate. Her dad talking to Piper, his pride evident in his smile.

"Who wants pumpkin pie?" Aunt Nora asks as she comes downstairs with a pumpkin pie in one hand and pecan in the other. Again Angie feels guilty. She could've carried more for Aunt Nora.

"I do!"

Angie turns and takes the pumpkin pie from Aunt Nora.

"Sorry guys, this one's all mine," she announces to her uncles.

"Like hell," Uncle Tom says with a laugh.

"It was worth a try."

"Next time hide it out on the deck," her cousin Brenna tells her, and they share a laugh over the year Brenna hid a coconut cream pie on Aunt Nora's deck. Her parents and aunts and uncles had moaned and groaned all evening about Aunt Janet forgetting to make the coconut cream pie, Aunt Janet had sworn she'd made it and brought it, and Brenna had been chased down the driveway later, coconut cream pie in hand.

"It's snowing." Angie shakes her head. "I'll have to just eat it all upstairs next time."

"C'mon, Nora," Uncle Tom says. "Cut the pie. Football game's on."

"Patience is a virtue," Aunt Nora answers. Again, it's all been said and done a million times before. But right now, missing her mom is an ache inside her, and Angie craves the comfort of hearing the banter a million more times.

6

L isa

SHE'D BEEN TOO BUSY TALKING TO JACK'S SISTERS AND nieces and helping with the finishing touches on dinner to think much about what was missing. *Who* was missing. In fact, much of the afternoon had gone the same as the day has always gone at home. Snacking and chatter and dinner preparations and then dinner itself. Wine. Turkey. Mashed potatoes. Pumpkin pie. More chatter and laughter. And then there had been the clean-up process, which involved dishwater, of course, but more wine, and more snitching pieces of turkey and another small piece of pie and more wine and talking and laughing.

But now, curled up against Jack in front of the fire in his sister's living room, Lisa remembers all that she'd given up this year. The turkey was good, but always at home—no matter if she were with Angie's family, Makenna's family, or Jamie's family—there was always turkey and ham. No one could make dressing like Brooke, and Lisa had never eaten apple pie better than Angie's.

It's not just the food, though, that Lisa feels sad about now. She misses her friends. She misses Makenna's bold, hard laugh that only escapes after she's had a few glasses of wine. She misses watching Jamie carve the turkey and the ham with an electric knife, reaching around him to grab a bite of both as he works. She wonders how Angie did this year without her mom. Last year had been so hard for her, Lisa had gone home that evening with such a heavy heart. She'd grown so used to not having a mom, but not Angie. Angie and her mom had always been close.

Lisa considers texting Angie, but she doesn't move. It's cozy here in front of the fire. She's warm and sleepy, and she lets her eyes close and just listens. Jack's nephews are in the den playing video games. The constant pattern of loud laughing and then excited talking is like a soundtrack to the moment. Lisa needs that soundtrack, because she misses the music Makenna is always playing through the whole holiday season.

There's got to be something wrong with her. Forty-year-old women shouldn't want to be with their friends. With their friends' families. Not on holidays. Lisa should have her own family by now. Only an epic failure—words she keps hearing from the boys down the hall—could be forty and have to borrow her friends' kids to spend time with them because she had none of her own.

Jack presses a kiss to the top of her head. He's getting sleepy, too. She can tell just from the way he's settling into the couch and the way his hand on her side is pulling her in closer against him. Alone with him for the moment, Lisa lets her mind go and imagines what it would be like to be with Jack for the rest of her life. To wear a wedding ring on her finger and to carry his child inside her. To carry his son on her hip and to braid his daughter's hair and dress her in fancy holiday dresses.

Why not? They fit together. They have fun. They laugh, and they talk. They both like peanut butter fudge, they both prefer the NHL to the NFL, and they both believe in God. They have more in common than they don't, although when they disagree on something, they talk it to death. They don't change each other's minds, but they enjoy the debate.

The sex is explosive and hot, and Lisa has wondered more than once if being single and having sex is better than being married and knowing she'd always be making love to the same man. She wonders if her friends' sex lives are as intense and enjoyable as her own.

Then again, she and Jack have been seeing each other for six months. Before Jack, she'd been with only two guys for at least eighteen months. Surely, her friends' have more consistency in their intimate lives. She doubts her friends sleep alone after making love, something she doesn't do often with Jack, but an experience she's had too often.

What would they think if they knew Jack is divorced? If they knew he has a sixteen-year-old daughter whom he rarely sees. Hell, she's not even sure what she thinks about it. She doesn't know that much about Jack's ex-wife or daughter. Just that the ex is now remarried, and though he's tried to get to know his daughter better, things just haven't worked out.

Why does her mind do this? Why, when she's so full and warm and content, does her mind take off like this? Why can't she just be here next to Jack? It could work. Does she love him? *Maybe.* She's not sure, but then she's only been with him six months. She'd council anyone to take more time than six months before jumping head first into a serious relationship and possibly a marriage.

She *could* love him. She knows this without doubt. He treats her like a princess, but he doesn't coddle her. She's not fragile. She's been on her own far too long to be fragile and dependent on a man. But she likes him. She likes to spend time with him.

But would he fit into her life? Would he like her friends? Would he be agreeable to spending holiday time and birthdays and plain old Saturday nights with her friends' families? And what about Jamie?

What about Jamie? Why does it matter? Would he like Jamie? Would Jamie like him?

Would bringing Jack into the fold be giving up on Jamie? Wait. Giving up on Jamie? He's married. Happily married. And he's never acted like anything more than a good friend and possibly a protective older brother.

The hell of it is she doesn't even know how she feels about that, about Jamie. She knows Makenna and Angie think she's in love with him. She has no idea what Jamie and Brooke think. There was a time when Lisa wanted so much to be the woman in Jamie's life, but she thinks she's beyond that now.

But then, if she were over any thoughts of Jamie, would she be sitting here in another man's arms, wondering what Jamie's doing right now?

"You know what I'm thinking?" Jack leans his head close to her again.

"Hmm?" She knows exactly what he's thinking, but she wants to hear him say it.

"I think we need to leave. And we need to go climb into that huge hotel bed and make love."

"I think we might lose each other in that huge bed," she says softly. But she tilts her head up and lets him kiss her.

"Trust me," he says with a smile. "I won't lose you."

"We've never made love in a hotel bed." She kisses the corner of his mouth. "Think it'll be different?"

"You know what I'd really like to do?" His fingers slide up over her side until he's touching the outside of her breast through her sweater.

Again, she knows exactly what he's going to say—doesn't that count for something?—but she wants him to say it.

"Tell me." She lifts her head from his shoulder to look at him.

"Undress you right here and make love by the fire."

A flame that has nothing to do with the fire climbs inside her.

"I'd like that."

"So would all those teenage boys just down the hall," Jack answers. Lisa laughs out loud.

"Please." She sits up straight. "It would scar them for life."

"No scars." He shakes his head. "But they'd never forget it."

When he kisses her, *really* kisses her, she leans so far into him that she's nearly in his lap. His hands are in her sweater, and hers are in his hair. She jumps away from him when they hear a particularly loud yell and laugh from down the hall. Jack mumbles that they really should leave, and Lisa agrees.

It occurs to her as they say their goodbyes and thank yous to his family that she never stopped to wonder if they liked her. Of course, she'd been nervous when they'd first arrived. But she'd jumped in right away to help and gotten caught up in conversation about the Black Friday sales and the new recipe for the dressing and a million other things, and she'd forgotten to be nervous. She'd forgotten she didn't know Jack's sisters, and they didn't know her, and she'd simply been herself and blended in anyway.

That's a good thing, she thinks as she and Jack hurry out to the SUV. It's gotten colder still, and the wind blows hard in her hair and takes away the last traces of warmth from the fireplace.

"I should've started it earlier to let it warm up," Jack says and blows on his hands.

"I thought you did," she answers with a grin.

He laughs as she rubs a hand over this thigh and lets it rest over his fly.

"With you, it never has a chance to cool off."

She raises her eyebrows. "And is that a problem?"

"Hell, no." His answer makes her laugh.

The drive to the hotel takes about fifteen minutes. Lisa glances at the clock. It's not quite ten. She wonders again about Angie and how she handled the day without her mom. If Angie and Makenna will shop tomorrow. She and Jack plan to join the crazy shoppers, but not at any ungodly hour. If they make love into the night, as they often do, they might not make any of those big door buster sales.

She doesn't care. In fact, at the moment, Lisa thinks she wouldn't mind staying in bed all day tomorrow, curled up with Jack. Making love with him is so consuming, she never has the time or desire to think of anyone else. Not even Jamie.

7

J amie

It's almost noon, and Brooke still isn't home. Jamie considers this fact for a moment and finally shrugs and goes back to the Christmas tree. Or the pieces that once put together will make their Christmas tree. He hadn't known Brooke had plans to shop, much less that she had plans to shop with Angie and Makenna. Not that it's a big deal. Gets him out of being in the middle of that insane rush of people, anyway.

Just too bad the boys couldn't drag themselves out of bed and help him with the tree. Whoever said it was a man's job anyway? Oh, he loves the tree once it's decorated. Too many good memories involving Christmas and a Christmas tree for him to not like it. He even likes the tree once he has the lights on. But the lights are just a pain in the ass.

He scratches his chin, remembers he hasn't shaved yet, and wonders again about Brooke out shopping with Angie and Makenna. They've been married for sixteen years, and they've always hung out with *his* friends. But he's not sure he's ever known his wife to spend time with any of them *on her own*. Hell, half the time he wonders if she really enjoys being around them or if she just puts on an act for him.

Of course, it would bother him if she didn't like them, if all these years she'd just been humoring him. He's as in love with Brooke today as he was sixteen years ago. He wants her to be happy, and yet, it would kill him if she suddenly announced that she wanted to move or that she didn't want to go to Makenna's for their Friends Thanks-giving or the Friends after Thanksgiving dinner at Angie and Brian's. And yet, he's never imagined Brooke jumping in the car by herself to meet Angie or Makenna or Lisa for coffee and shopping.

Lisa. He misses her. Probably he's better off not sharing that with Brooke, but there's nothing more to it. Lisa has been an extension of himself for so many years that he kind of finds it hard to function when she's not around. Like putting up this damned tree with a broken arm. He knows by now that Lisa went out of town for the holiday with a guy. Jack Holloman. He doesn't know Jack well, though they've met at the school. He'd known, of course, that Lisa had gone out with him. But he had no idea how serious they'd gotten.

He hasn't really given it much thought. It's just going to be weird at Angie and Brian's tomorrow night without

Lisa around. It'll work though, because Brooke will be with him. And it's always a good time. He'll miss Lisa's peanut butter cookies; she'd started making them for him when they were sophomores in high school. He hated chocolate chip, and peanut butter were his favorite. So Brooke made the boys chocolate chip cookies, and Lisa made him his favorite, and everyone was happy.

Is Brooke happy? He stills his hands on the branches as he wonders about his wife. He thinks so. He thinks they have a good, solid marriage, with enough adventure and laughter that neither of them should be bored or unhappy. True, Brooke has been talking about going back to work. That's okay by him. Hell, he doesn't even care that she applied at the school. She'd be a good school nurse. But she'd gotten prickly about it the other day when they talked about it.

Prickly about the school. And him. And Lisa.

Whatever, he decides, as he begins winding the lights through the tree limbs. From time to time, Brooke has worried about his feelings for Lisa. He's never given her reason to doubt him, and he won't, but he gets frustrated whenever that green monster possesses his wife.

Sometimes Brooke seems determined to make him aware of how alluring Lisa is. Yes, dammit, she's gorgeous, and she's sexy. He loves her laugh, and yes, he loves her. He loves Lisa; he always has. But he's not in love with her. Some days his wife plays dumb, as if she doesn't get the difference.

He hadn't seen her shopping list today. Hell, she'd rolled out of bed at dark-thirty and jumped in the shower before he'd known what was going on. He's still not sure what time she left the house. He'd been in and out of a dream involving a math problem one of his students couldn't understand. Probably too much leftover turkey before he'd gone to bed. But he's not sure if the turkey or the math problem had given him heartburn.

Once he'd gotten up and showered, though, he was fine. He'd even fixed breakfast and hollered for the boys to come out and eat with him. The promise of food is usually enough to rouse them, especially Daniel. That kid is growing like a weed. Jamie hates clichés, but that one is true. Brooke has a hell of a time keeping Daniel in pants long enough for him. Daniel would rather wear shorts when it's two degrees outside than wear any pair of pants that might be high waters.

Neither kid had joined him for breakfast. Jamie had even gone upstairs to check on them, but he'd found them both out cold in their respective bedrooms. Daniel's feet hung off the end of his bed, his face half-buried under his pillow. Jared slept on his side, curled up in a tight ball. Jamie had almost knocked loudly on their doors to rouse them. His father would have done it. But he'd decided against it and walked away quietly, letting them sleep in.

He has no idea what either of them wants for Christmas this year. Something expensive, he's sure, because what else is there for boys their age? Brooke would probably get them a couple of new video games. That was okay with him, because the boys didn't spend that much time playing them. They were outdoor guys, all the way. Sports fanatics, which suited Jamie just fine.

Hmm. Was Brooke out there getting something for him? He wanted a new chainsaw, but he hadn't mentioned it to her. Maybe she'd just gone to get out for a bit. It did seem to be getting to her, staying cooped up in the house all day every day.

He can't help but wonder if she'd have gone if Lisa was with them. Probably. As far as he can tell, even though Brooke has her occasional bouts of jealousy, she likes Lisa. In fact, he remembers now that Lisa had been at his house the other night. Sitting at the kitchen table with Brooke, talking until well after midnight. He and the boys had been watching TV. He'd gone to bed around midnight, and Brooke and Lisa had still been yakking away in the kitchen.

"'s cold in here."

Jamie looks up from the tree to see Jared, his youngest, stumble around the corner of the steps and into the living room.

"'Bout time you got up," Jamie tells him. "It's after noon."

"Can't believe you didn't drag me 'n' Daniel out of bed."

"I should've." Jamie eyes the lights to see if they're spaced well enough on the tree. "I lost track of time working on this damned thing."

"Mom says you're not supposed to cuss the tree," Jared reminds him. "I'm hungry."

"Bacon in the fridge."

"You made bacon?" Jared yawns and scratches his head. Jamie notices that Jared looks like he's grown a few inches taller.

"Yep."

"Can I have a piece of pie?"

Jamie looks up again to see Jared eyeballing the leftover pecan pie on the counter.

"Instead of bacon?"

"Mm."

"Sure."

Within seconds, Daniel joins them downstairs. Unlike Jared, he's never talkative in the morning. Through the open layout of the house, Jamie half-watches as he gets out the bacon and warms it in the microwave. Jared pours himself a glass of milk, and Daniel chooses orange juice.

"Where's Mom?" Daniel asks, his mouth full of bacon and bread.

"Don't talk with your mouth full," Jamie tells him, and he knows before Jared says so that he sounds just like Brooke.

"Right there." Jared laughs and points at Jamie. Daniel grins.

"Shopping."

"Really?" Daniel raises his eyebrows. "I thought she hated getting up early."

"I think she's bored staying home all the time," Jamie answers. He holds his breath for a minute and wonders if he shouldn't have said that. Maybe Brooke's boredom and her need to get out of the house and go back to work should be a family discussion.

"Who'd she go with?" Jared asks. "Grandma hates shopping on Red Friday."

"It's Black Friday, stupid," Daniel informs him.

"Daniel." Jamie gives him a stern look. "Don't talk to your brother that way. Jared, she's with Angie and Makenna."

"Lisa didn't go?"

"She's in Champagne with that guy," Daniel reminds his brother.

"Oh yeah. Her new boyfriend."

"He's not her boyfriend, is he, Dad?" Daniel asks Jamie.

"Huh?" Jamie looks over at them from the tree. "Yeah, he's her boyfriend."

"Yeah, she wouldn't go to someone else's Thanksgiving if he wasn't her boyfriend, would she?" Jared gives Daniel a look that seems to say he finally knows something Daniel doesn't.

Daniel shrugs carelessly and yawns. "Wonder what Mom's getting. She shopping for me 'n Jared?"

"I have no idea," Jamie answers honestly. "I think I heard her say Santa was bringing you guys rocks this year, so probably not."

Both boys laugh. When the phone rings, Jared nearly tips his chair over as he jumps to answer it.

"H'llo?" Jared walks the phone over to his dad. "It's Mom. Tell her I want that new video game."

"Yeah, that's really helpful," Daniel mumbles.

"Hey." Jamie turns back to the tree, the phone pinned between his ear and shoulder.

"Hi. Whatcha doing?"

"Working on the tree." He reaches up to spread more branches. "What's going on?"

"We're going to lunch. Called to see if you wanna go."

Going to lunch? Jamie wonders. "You and Makenna and Angie?"

"Mm-hmm."

"Guys, you wanna go to lunch with mom and Makenna and Ang?"

"No," Daniel answers immediately.

"Huh-uh."

Jamie laughs. "I think we're gonna find something

here. I'm gonna make these guys help me with the outside lights."

"Cool," Jared says and nods.

"And then we're gonna shoot some baskets," Daniel tells Jared. "Prepare to be amazed."

"Actually, I'm pretty amazing myself."

Jamie rolls his eyes. "Brooke, the guys and I are gonna stay home today. You have fun, though."

"Okay." She sounds out of breath. Jamie wonders how crazy it is out there with the obsessed Black Friday shoppers. He shivers, glad to be at home, out of the cold and away from the crowds. "I'll be home later."

"Isn't that kind of weird?" Daniel asks when Jamie hangs up the phone.

"Isn't what kind of weird?"

"Mom doing lunch with Angie and Makenna. Without Lisa."

Jamie starts to say yes, it is kind of weird. But then, he decides maybe it's not so weird. Maybe Brooke enjoys Makenna and Angie's company, but she finds it hard to be comfortable around Lisa. His mind flashes on the image of Lisa and Brooke, at the kitchen table, talking the other night. Okay, maybe that theory is crap, and he really has no idea what to think about Brooke and their friends.

"Get dressed, guys," he tells them and avoids commenting on Brooke's shopping trip. "We've got a lot to do today."

8

M akenna

It's been a great day, which surprises Makenna both because she's not usually into the Black Friday madness and Lisa's not with them. She'd been surprised the other day when Angie had called her and told her she'd invited Brooke to go shopping with them. First, she'd told Angie that she had no plans to go shopping early Black Friday, and then when Angie had told her in no uncertain terms that she would be going shopping, she'd asked Angie why she'd invited Brooke.

"Because she's fun," Angie had answered. "And why shouldn't we invite her?"

They'd stood in line for over an hour at an electronics store, but Makenna doesn't mind. Angie had gotten Brian a new iPad, and Brooke had picked up smart phones for both of her boys, and Makenna got her girls both hand-held electronic games. The savings there alone had been worth getting out of bed early. Angie'd found four CDs Piper wanted, so she'd bought two and Makenna and Brooke both bought one for her, too. Makenna had dragged them all out of the store when Angie stopped to look at the e-reader devices. Angie had been considering getting Piper one, but Makenna knew she wasn't sure about it. Probably after the iPad for Brian, she didn't care to buy the reader. Only so much one credit card can take in one day.

They'd gone to a local discount store, where they'd bought more CDs, a couple of video games, and wrapping paper. The mall, where they'd each found a few things to mark off their lists. By noon they were all hungry, so deciding lunch was the next stop was easy.

Waiting at the bar of McGee's, a favored local bar and grill, the three of them sip their drinks and relive their shopping rushes of the day. Makenna notices Angie has gotten quiet. She watches her friend twist her wine glass in slow circles on the bar.

"Hey." Makenna nudges Angie's leg with her own. "You okay?"

Angie nods, but she doesn't look away from the red wine, gently swirling in the glass.

"It doesn't go away," Brooke says softly, "but it does get a little easier each year."

Angie blinks and turns to Brooke. Makenna wonders for a moment who Brooke thinks she is. When she remembers that Brooke's dad had passed away five years ago, just before Christmas, she takes a deep breath and looks away. She stares at the top of a whiskey bottle and wonders how in the hell she could have forgotten that. What kind of friend would forget that?

Not a close friend, that's for sure, she tells herself. And then it hits her that she's not really a close friend to Brooke and she knows exactly why she's not, and suddenly guilt reams her on both sides. It squeezes her painfully tight; the guilt for never letting Brooke in and the guilt for thinking that they should let Brooke into their circle, no matter what Lisa feels or doesn't feel for Brooke's husband.

"Thank you," Angie tells Brooke. "Sometimes I think about her so much, it's like she's with me everywhere. And sometimes…."

Brooke picks up where Angie left off, "Sometimes you go days at a time and forget to think about him, and then you catch yourself having fun, and you realize you haven't thought of him at all, and the guilt eats you up."

Angie nods. Though Makenna's lost family members through the years, her parents are both healthy, so she feels like she can't contribute to this conversation.

"Would your mom want you to be happy, Ang?" Brooke takes a sip of her mixed drink. Makenna's never seen Brooke drink more than a beer or two at their get-togethers. She finds it interesting that Brooke ordered an amaretto sour.

"Sure she would," Angie answers. The noise in the bar is phenomenal, and Angie's voice is small and quiet, but Makenna hears her loud and clear. "I tell myself there's a time and place to remember." Angie shrugs. "But some-times I don't listen very well."

"It's okay." Brooke shakes her head and offers Angie a smile. "There's no rulebook on how to do it."

"How's your mom doing?" Angie asks Brooke, and Makenna sees the grief slide off her shoulders. Angie does not wallow. Makenna has never seen Angie slide into depression or self-pity. She feels things to the core: happiness, grief, anger, but she never wallows. Those emotions light her eyes often, but they steal away almost as quickly as they come.

"She's doing well. Thanks for asking." Brooke nods.

The hostess calls for Hodges, table for three, so they gather their purses and drinks and follow the young girl to a corner table.

"Do you guys think I should get Piper an e-reader?" Angie asks when they are seated. Makenna and Brooke sit across from Angie and put their purses next to her, since she has more room.

"As much as she reads?" Brooke asks, and again, Makenna wonders about her. Of course she'd know Piper as well as any of them, since Jamie and Brooke have always been a part of their lives. "I think it'd be a great gift."

"She's out of room on her bookshelf," Angie says with a nod, as if she thinks she will get one for Piper.

"Like mother, like daughter." Makenna smiles sweetly. "Right?"

"We love books." Angie shrugs, but she laughs. "It's not just about reading. It's about the feel of the book in your hand."

"So?" Makenna takes a long drink of her beer. "No e-reader? Just books?"

"I don't know!" Angie groans and drags her fingers back through her dark auburn hair.

"Wasn't it easier to shop for them when they were little?" Brooke sounds wistful. "I never know what to get the boys now. They like video games, but they're happiest outside. Shooting baskets or throwing a football."

"And there are only so many new footballs you need, right?" Makenna says with a nod. "It is easier when they're little."

"Piper's easy." Brooke leans back against the booth.

"Right. E-reader or not." Brooke tilts her head a bit. Makenna has to laugh. Sounds just like something she'd have said.

"Yeah, but she didn't ask for it. She'd be happy with clothes."

Their waiter appears and takes their orders. They're all hungry, and they pass on lady-like salads and order burgers and fries.

Makenna laughs when the waiter walks away. "Wouldn't the guys laugh at us? Hitting the alcohol and eating grease."

"I'm starved," Brooke answers. "I didn't eat breakfast."

"Neither did I."

"Shame on you guys." Makenna tucks her hair behind her ear and grins. "I had a big piece of apple pie for breakfast."

"Have either of you talked to Lisa?" Brooke asks. Surprised by the question, Makenna looks to Angie to answer it. Seems like after nearly twenty years, they shouldn't have to worry about this. Apparently it isn't weird for Jamie, Brooke, and Lisa.

"I talked to her the night before Thanksgiving." Angie's

answer is smooth. So smooth that Makenna has to wonder if Angie has dismissed the curiosity and the suspicions about Lisa's feelings for Jamie. True, she and Angie don't spend hours at a time talking about it. But still. Makenna can't help but wonder if Lisa will ever be happily in love with someone else.

"She called me last night," Makenna says. "They were at Jack's sister's house."

"Is she having fun?"

Makenna glances at Brooke and decides to take a page from Angie's book. Forget the whole love triangle thing, because maybe it just plain doesn't exist. Maybe all these years she has been painting this picture to be much more dramatic than it is.

"Yeah, it sounded like it. Sounded like what she's used to. Lots of people. Lots of kids."

Makenna stops when she sees the look on Brooke's face. A look of...knowing? No, not really. To Makenna, that would imply smugness, and she doesn't think Brooke is like that. Maybe just understanding?

"Then she is having fun."

"What do you mean?" Angie asks. She looks up as the waiter approaches with their meals on a tray. Brooke waits until their plates are in front of them and they are alone again before she speaks.

"The kids. Lisa probably loved being with the kids."

Makenna and Angie don't answer right away. They busy themselves loading their burgers with ketchup, mustard, and pickles.

"Lisa hated not being with our kids," Brooke gestures around the table to say she meant all of their kids, "this year. She probably misses them more than she misses any of us."

True, Lisa has always loved their kids, all of them. But it seems odd for Brooke to point this out as the first thing Lisa would enjoy this holiday. What about Jack's company? Meeting his family?

"She's never talked to you about this, has she?" Brooke mumbles.

"Talked to us about what?" Angie goes still, and she stares at Brooke, waiting for an answer.

Brooke sighs. "She's feeling that biological clock ticking."

"What?" Makenna shakes her head. *Lisa Fairchild? Wants a baby? No way.*

"Lisa wants to have her own children."

"Lisa? *Our* Lisa?" Angie asks, and Makenna swallows down some guilt with her cheeseburger. She's kind of glad that Angie doesn't seem to know any more about this than she does.

"She's the professional in our group. Sexy, single. Always doing more at school. More responsibility. More involvement with the…" Angie's words slow. She looks at Makenna.

"She told you that?" Makenna asks Brooke. "Lisa told you she wants a baby?"

Brooke nods slowly. "I wondered if she'd ever talked to you guys about it."

"Why wouldn't she talk to us about it?" Angie asks, clearly puzzled. "I mean…why not tell all of us?"

"I need another drink." Brooke rattles the ice in her glass.

"No, it's okay." Angie recovers herself and shakes her head. "You don't have to tell us. Lisa confided in you."

Brooke shakes her head. "It's not you she wanted to keep it from. She doesn't want Jamie to know what she's going through right now."

"Going through," Makenna repeats. "Going through? Like she's not just talking about it? She's going through something?"

"No, no, no," Brooke says quickly. "No, not like that. She just wants..." She takes a deep breath and shakes her head. "I've said too much."

"No, you can't just not tell us now." Angie reaches across the table and touches Brooke's hand.

"And where does it leave me when she's pissed because I told you something she said to me?"

"Right here with us." Angie squeezes her hand. "Now I wish Lisa were here. Sounds like we have things to talk about."

"If Lisa were here, I wouldn't be," Brooke says matter-of-factly. Makenna twists in her seat, suddenly feeling like they're in junior high again.

"What's that mean?" she asks quickly.

"That you three would be hanging out. Probably not shopping. And I wouldn't be with you. I'd be at home with Jamie and the boys."

"By choice, though?" Makenna pushes to clarify what Brooke is saying, even though she knows she shouldn't.

"Makenna, when's the last time the three of us have gotten together for a day of shopping and lunch?"

Angie's giggle is low and infectious. Makenna throws a French fry at her.

"She's right." Angie shrugs. She takes the fry Makenna threw at her and dips it in ketchup.

"Throw that at me, and die," Makenna warns her.

"I'm not scared, I'm hungry," Angie tells her as she pops the fry into her mouth. "You're right, Brooke. We don't invite you to do this stuff with us. I'm sorry."

"Don't apologize. I'm not complaining. It's just the way it's always been. I come with Jamie. And I'm out with my family and friends a lot." Brooke takes a bite of her burger. Makenna had forgotten about her own burger. For a minute, her stomach had been trying to tell her she wasn't hungry. Now that the storm may have passed, the hunger returns.

"I don't think Lisa meant to tell me anything," Brooke continues. "Do you know what I mean? She was over at the house for dinner one night a couple of weeks ago. After dinner, we cleaned the kitchen. The boys were in and out, and Lisa was giving them grief about homework and girls and stuff. And then she and I got to talking about the boys and then our own school years. Before we knew it, it was almost midnight. The boys were in bed. Jamie went to bed. We sat there and talked."

"And she said she wanted to have a baby."

Brooke studies Makenna's face for a few seconds and then she nods helplessly. "Yes. She said that."

"So." Angie drinks the last of the wine in her glass and considers Brooke's story. "So, what's she going through? Is she depressed about this? I mean, has it become that big of a deal, and Makenna and I never even noticed?"

"Kind of." Brooke purses her lips. "I think it's more that Lisa's done that good of a job of hiding it."

"But why hide it?" Makenna asks. "Why hide it from us?"

"Don't you think it's sometimes easier to let go and say things to someone you don't know that well? To someone who doesn't know everything about you?"

"Like maybe we all hide something from everyone? Even our closest friends?" Angie frowns. She looks around, and Makenna knows she wants another glass of wine.

"Maybe," Brooke answers, but she shakes her head. "I think Lisa feels inferior to you both."

"What?" Makenna squeezes her eyes shut. "Call her. Put her on speakerphone."

Angie barks a loud laugh. "Might get more than we bargained for, Makenna. She's with Jack, remember."

Makenna takes a slow, deep breath through her nose and then looks at Angie and then Brooke. "Sex? Afternoon sex? God, what is that like?"

"Pretty damned fun," Brooke answers.

"Do tell." Makenna tilts her head to study Brooke. They laugh, but the seriousness of their discussion soon intrudes on the moment of fun.

"Why would we make her feel inferior? She's our best friend."

"Ang, you don't make her feel that way. I mean, it's nothing either of you guys do."

"Nothing intentional, you mean," Makenna says softly.

Brooke nods.

Makenna looks at Angie. "We've both been married for years. And we both have children. And we both work."

Angie looks at Brooke. "Is that it?"

Brooke hesitates, but she answers with a small nod.

"She especially doesn't want to talk about any of this with Jamie."

"Because he's married and has children," Angie guesses.

"It's always a little more complicated than that with Lisa and Jamie, isn't it?" Brooke's words come out in a harsh whisper.

"I need another beer," Makenna mumbles and turns to look for their waiter.

ngie

"Wait." Angie picks up her empty wine glass and then sets it down again. "Did you just say…"

She feels Brooke looking at her, and then Makenna's looking at her, and she wonders why the hell they expect her to take the lead here. Brooke is the one who just climbed on top of the elephant that has been in the middle of every room they've ever stood in since Brooke and Jamie got married. Why not let Brooke handle it?

She can't avoid both sets of eyes forever, and she finally gives in and looks at Makenna, who is suddenly deathly pale.

"I really need more wine," Angie groans.

"Guys." Brooke shakes her head and reaches out to

touch Angie's hand, which is again playing with her wine glass. "Relax. I didn't mean *that*."

"What did you mean?" Makenna finds her voice. Angie sighs in relief and flops back in the booth.

"Well, I think we all know that if Jamie and I weren't married, he'd be with Lisa."

Makenna slides back into herself and drops her chin to her chest. Angie watches her drag her fingers through her hair and silently thanks her for leaving her hanging out to dry again.

"I don't really think so," Angie tells Brooke. She knows Makenna believes that what Brooke just said is true, but Angie really doesn't think so. For one thing, she's always seen so much more of the friendship in Jamie and Lisa's relationship that anything else sort of fades into the background. Besides, Jamie's obviously very much in love with Brooke and very happy with her, so Angie really hasn't allowed herself to consider what might be if there were no Brooke in the equation.

"Makenna." Brooke circles her fingers around Makenna's wrist. "Stop with the heart attack stuff. I know there's nothing going on with Lisa and Jamie. I know they're not sleeping together. I know they never have."

"Never?" Angie asks before she can stop herself. She feels a deep blush climb to her face, and she hates herself for asking. "I just...I guess I've wondered if they ever messed around when they were younger. You know. Friends with benefits."

"That phrase didn't exist when we were kids," Makenna tells Angie.

Angie glares at her but turns back to look at Brooke.

"I mean," she clears her throat and forces herself to look Brooke in the eye, "Lisa's always sworn nothing ever happened. I just always wondered."

"Jamie said there's never been anything between them. I believe him."

Angie wonders if she'd believe Brian if he were best friends with a woman and swore to her nothing had ever happened between them.

"So. I don't get why you said that. About things being complicated with Lisa and Jamie."

Brooke looks at Makenna again. "He's in love with her."

"No." Angie shakes her head. "No, Brooke, he's not. He's in love with you, and even a blind man could see that."

"This isn't about me, Ang. I'm not saying that Jamie doesn't love me. I'm saying Jamie's in love with Lisa. He always has been."

"So, Jamie loves you both?" Makenna asks. Angie looks up when their waiter approaches the table. She wants to throw herself on the guy's mercy and beg for the bottle of wine, but she controls herself and merely asks for a second glass. Makenna and Brooke also order another drink.

"You don't believe a person can be in love with more than one person at a time?"

Angie raises her eyebrows when Brooke turns back to look at her. "I don't know. I guess it's an uncomfortable thought, so I don't let myself go there."

Brooke shrugs. "Jamie's in love with her. I think she loves him, but I think she's trying hard not to be in love with him. To find someone else."

They hold their conversation when the waiter comes back with their drinks. Angie takes a healthy drink of her wine before she speaks again.

"So, you're okay with this? You think Jamie is in love with her and married to you. They're friends, and they work together, and you're okay with this."

"Yeah," Brooke answers. "I mean, I'd rather he didn't love her, but I think a part of him always will."

"But, Brooke." Makenna twists sideways in their side of the booth to study Brooke. "He could have had Lisa. He chose to spend his life with you."

"I know." Brooke nods. "Look, I didn't mean to throw a monkey wrench into a good day. I just...things are anything but simple between Jamie and Lisa. That's all I meant. Please don't take anything I said the wrong way."

Angie wonders what's to take the wrong way. If Brooke truly believes Jamie's in love with another woman, then she's taking the high road.

"You have a bond with Jamie that no one can break," Makenna says softly. Angie watches her touch Brooke's wedding band. "And I don't mean this. You gave Jamie two sons. No one can take that away from you."

Brooke hesitates and then smiles and nods. Makenna doesn't seem to notice, but Angie wonders exactly what Brooke is thinking.

Angie drinks more wine. She wonders what Lisa is doing and if she's enjoying herself, but she knows better than to go down that road right now.

"I wonder what my crew's doing at home." She covers a yawn and then smiles. "I think I'm gonna need a nap."

Brooke's eyes meet her own, and Angie sees the thank you written all over her face. She wonders what about this conversation became too much for Brooke to take if it wasn't talking about Jamie being in love with Lisa Fairchild.

10

L isa

THE WEEKEND HAD BEEN SO ENJOYABLE SHE DIDN'T EVEN care that she had a stack of tests to grade when she got home. Jack had carried her bags in for her, and she'd been about to suggest a glass of wine or even a cup of cocoa. But then she'd spotted the stack of tests on the kitchen table, and the flashing light on her answering machine had reminded her that she had messages from all of her friends that she should return. Nothing like a Sunday evening, all alone, grading papers. But then again, she hadn't had a Thanksgiving weekend quite like this one in years, so it was all worth it.

Jack had graciously said good night, not-so-graciously kissed her goodnight (which almost changed her mind about sending him away) and left her alone. Rather than call her friends, she'd texted all of them to say she'd had a great trip, she was home, but had to grade some tests, and she'd talk to all of them tomorrow.

It was a cop-out. She'd known it when she'd sent the texts, and she'd known they would all see through it. But she wasn't ready to talk about the holiday, about Jack. As much as she enjoyed the family day with him, and as much fun as they had shopping together on Friday, as intimate as she and Jack had been sharing the shower and getting ready together, not to mention making love, she still wasn't sure what was going on. If she loved him.

She wasn't sure if she missed Jamie. Or if she felt like she was *supposed* to miss Jamie.

Today, though, there will be no avoiding any of them. Jamie is just down the hall in his classroom, and Lisa knows any minute, after the bell rings and the kids race to their lockers to head home, he will wander in to talk. The talk with Jamie won't have the same tone the talks with Angie and Makenna will. He'll question her about Jack and his family, but it'll be all big-brother like, which she finds irritating. It used to make her feel good knowing that he cared enough to be involved, but since she'd turned thirty-five and started feeling the urge to settle down and have her own family, Jamie's concern has felt more like interference.

Angie and Makenna will quiz her on Jack and his family, but they'll want to know how he compares to Jamie, if Lisa's in love with him. If she were to say that she is, they'll test her. They'll examine her and her feelings like a specimen under a microscope, because no matter what she does, they seem determined that she's deeply in love with and pining away for Jamie.

They mean well. They all mean well, and Lisa knows this. But good intentions sometimes pave the way to hell, and Lisa would really like to be left alone with all of this. Whether she's in love with Jamie or not, she just needs a break—a mental health break—to figure it out.

She feels the sting of guilt when she realizes she'd rather talk to Brooke about Jack than any of them. They aren't in junior high school anymore, but she knows Angie and Makenna will be hurt if they find out she's talked to Brooke about some of this stuff. She blows out a deep breath in a frustrated huff and then drags her fingers through her hair.

Hard to not feel this way when the whole group of them have lived in each other's pockets for so many years. She's not ready to walk away and change her life that drastically. And yet, she really needs to think for herself and make her own decisions. Convincing her friends that she's capable of doing just that seems impossible.

"Hey."

Lisa hears the smile in his voice. Still sitting at her desk, she turns and looks up at Jamie. In his black Chinos and blue pullover, he looks casual and warm. His smile lights up his face and gives her hope that he hasn't come to Jack bash.

"Hi."

"Welcome home." He shoves his hands into his pockets and slouches against the doorframe. "How was your Thanksgiving?"

"Thank you." Lisa leans back in her chair and folds her arms over her chest. "It was great, actually. I really enjoyed it."

"Good."

"I missed you guys, though."

"We missed you," he says quietly, but he's still smiling. "But I'm glad you had a good time."

Lisa watches him for signs that he's lying or that there's a *but* coming.

"Jack's sister makes a killer pecan pie. I think I gained five pounds just from dinner."

He raises his eyebrows. "Really? You ate delicious pecan pie and didn't bring me any? And now you're going to add insult to injury by telling me about it?"

"I got the recipe."

"Yeah?" he perks up. "And you'll make it for me?"

"I'll attempt it."

"Awesome." He nods. "Brooke did something different with the dressing this year. Freakin' incredible."

Lisa grins. Every year Jamie and the guys eat enough to fill a horse and claim it was the best dinner ever. She did miss them.

But she did enjoy her time away with Jack.

"The girls went shopping," Jamie tells her. "Ang and Kenna and Brooke. Went out for lunch. Had a few drinks. Brooke came home and crashed. She slept for a couple of hours."

"Really?" Uh-oh. The three of them shopping. Having lunch. Having drinks. She knows she's probably in trouble. But then again, maybe not. She'd trusted Brooke for a reason. Why assume she'd break that trust the first chance she had?

"She said they missed you."

"Jack and I spent Friday shopping."

"As long as you didn't get up at three a.m. to get the good deals."

"Have you ever known me to get up at three a.m. for anything?"

"Good point." He nods. "I have known you to stay out until three, though."

"Did that Saturday night. Went to dinner and then went to a club."

"Do some dancin', did ya?" Jamie asks as he stands up straight and starts moving to music only he can hear.

"We did."

"Now that sounds like fun." He grins at her. "We should all go out New Year's Eve. Dinner and drinks. A little dancing."

She smiles wistfully, because it does sound like fun. But she thinks putting Jamie and Jack at a dinner table together might be pushing it. She's not even sure how Jack would feel about hanging out with her friends.

"Ask Jack," Jamie tells her as if he sees her thoughts. "I'll see what Brooke thinks."

"Sure. I will."

"By the way, my boys missed you," he says as he steps out of her room. "They said NFL Sunday isn't the same without you."

Her laughter bubbles up from deep inside. "That's because they rip me off for at least five bucks every week!"

"Oh, yeah." Jamie sticks his head back in. "They said to tell you that you owe 'em five."

"Tell 'em gambling is illegal in this school—"

"No gambling, ma'am," Jamie calls over his shoulder as he walks away. "I'm just the messenger."

Lisa stares at the open lesson plan book on her desk. A ghost of a smile still touches her lips. She likes hockey better, but she loves watching football with Daniel and Jared, even if she does lose ninety percent of the bets they make. Even if they do try to wheedle out of those bets when they lose. Well, they used to. Now that they're older, they usually pay up.

She can't just change everything. She can't just walk away from everything she's known for Jack. These guys are her family. Does that mean she's in love with Jamie Maczum? No.

What about the way her heart had skipped and touched her stomach with butterfly wings when Jamie had walked in just now? Did that mean she was in love with him? Still?

11

Makenna

THE FIRST DECEMBER SNOW IS SOMEHOW PRETTIER AND more exciting than November snow. Makenna steps away from her desk and looks out the office window to watch the soft, fat flakes float to the ground. Cold air touches her, and she lays a hand on the windowsill. It's cold, and for a minute, Makenna feels like she's standing out in the yard.

She reaches back and grabs her coffee mug from the desk. Her Mariah Carey Christmas CD is playing, and she likes it. But at the moment, she thinks Dean Martin and "Marshmallow World" would be more appropriate. She'll curse the snow later when she has to leave the house to get the girls from school, but for now she simply enjoys it.

When Dan Duncan had predicted snow on the local

weather report last night, the girls started praying for a snow day. Since they couldn't talk Dave into wearing his pajamas inside out, they'd flushed ice cubes down the toilet (they each flushed two) and slept with spoons under their pillows. Neither ritual had brought the hoped for snow day.

However—Makenna presses her forehead to the window and looks at the light blanket of snow that already covers the ground—it if keeps snowing like this, maybe they'll get a snow day tomorrow. Makenna decides she wouldn't mind that. It's early in the season, and she doesn't have a lot of stuff she can have the girls help her wrap, but there are a few things, and they could make cookies or watch Christmas movies.

She laughs at herself when she realizes she's thinking like Ariel and Aidyn now.

"Back to work, Makenna," she groans aloud. She takes her mug to the kitchen for a refill and decides to change the music while she's out here. She loves the contemporary music, even "Christmas Wrapping" by The Waitresses, but right now she's in the mood for something traditional. She chooses Bing Crosby, snags her mug from the counter, and goes back to her office.

She doesn't go back to work, though. The snow outside calls to her. It's funny how certain songs or even certain ornaments make her think of specific Christmas memories. Makenna is well aware that she's blessed with a full, happy life. Her grandparents have all passed away, but she's never suffered the loss of a parent.

The tree in the corner of the office draws her attention from the snow outside. Coffee mug still in hand, she squats down to look at the ornaments and the two presents that lay on the green and red plaid skirt. She doesn't know how Angie got through the first year without her mom. The first minute. The first day. The first Christmas. Any Christmas to come.

Makenna takes a small drink of her coffee and reaches out to finger an ornament. It's shiny and round, with a cavity inside it that shines even more. These were her grandma's ornaments, her grandma on her dad's side. She'd always loved them when she was a little girl, and she counts herself lucky to have gotten them when Grandma died two years ago.

She tilts the ornament to watch it reflect the light, but she's not really looking at it. Instead, she's thinking about her grandma. They'd been really close when she was a little girl. Makenna had spent many nights at Grandma's house, and she probably remembers them all, though they kind of overlap in her mind. But the Christmas memories are some of the best. Grandma's tree had been a little on the scrawny side, but she'd never noticed when she was a little girl.

Grandma always had dinner at her house on Christmas Eve, and Makenna's aunts and uncles and cousins would all be there. They'd eat baked ham and mashed potatoes and pie. Grandma made the best pie, didn't even matter what kind she made. There was always Christmas music, but it was just the radio playing from the spare bedroom. They'd all gather around the tree after the kitchen was clean (Makenna and her cousins had always helped clean things up) and open presents. At Grandma's house, they each got three or four presents—a far cry from how things are for her own daughters—but those three or four presents were always enough. Dolls.

Doll clothes. Sometimes games. One year, Santa brought Makenna's cousin a puppy. They'd brought the puppy, which they'd named Scully, to Grandma's house. Scully had been the life of the party, and Grandma hadn't even gotten mad when he got rough under the tree and broke an ornament.

The ornament comes back into focus, and Makenna feels her knees aching from squatting for so long. She'd never dreamed of what forty would be like, and now in less than twelve months, she'll know what forty is. Already, she doesn't like it. With one hand she reaches forward to straighten the packages under the tree, and then she stands and refuses to listen to her bones creak and pop.

It's time to get back to work, but she has no desire to sit down and get at it. She'd rather stand here and watch the snow or stare at the tree. Actually, she wouldn't mind stretching out on the couch for a nap. But she can't. The Christmas cards for Nina Andrews' business need to be printed, and she still has seven posters to plan and print for clients.

She sets her mug down on the coaster on her desk, stretches, and thinks about Angie at work at the bank. Every great once in a while, especially during the holiday season, Makenna misses being out and about and working with the general public. The holidays are usually a fun time, and office life can be especially fun at Christmas time. But mostly, she's thrilled to work out of her own home, alone and in charge of her day.

She thinks about Lisa struggling to control a classroom full of kids before Christmas. Doesn't matter how old they are, Makenna's sure there's no classroom full of kids that would be easy to handle just before a big break.

Speaking of Lisa, she thinks, she hasn't really had time to catch up with her since her trip to Champagne with Jack. She thinks about calling Angie or even just texting her. But she really doesn't have the time right now. The cards and the posters really need to be done ASAP. She'd hated that saying when she was out in the work force, but now that she is her own boss and her business depends on customer satisfaction, she lives by the phrase.

Maybe they can get together later this week. Go out for dinner or at least a drink. Angie's probably just as anxious to hear about Lisa's weekend as she is. Maybe Jack's the one. If that's the case, Makenna would like to get to know him better.

12

L isa

ANGIE HAD CALLED HER TWICE EARLIER IN THE WEEK, BUT she'd been too busy to talk long. Angie had asked about her Thanksgiving with Jack, and Lisa had only said they'd had a good time. Probably Angie and Makenna know she's holding back. *Probably, hell.* They both know her inside and out, and they know she's been busy all this fall laying bricks in a wall to keep them out. She's not being fair to them, but she can't seem to stop what she's doing. She doesn't want to hurt them, and she doesn't want the dynamics of their friendship to change. It's just kind of hard to talk to them about everything they have and everything she doesn't have. They don't judge her; she knows they don't. But sometimes she feels like they do. Lisa never measures up in her own eyes when she compares herself to Angie or Makenna, and sometimes that voice in her head is so loud and hard to ignore.

What's unforgivable or would be, if they knew, is that she's talking to Brooke. Again. She's comfortable at the Maczum's kitchen table, hands curled around a mug of hot chocolate, talking to Brooke about all of this stuff on her mind. The stuff that's giving her the mother of all headaches.

Why would she suddenly feel more comfortable sitting with Brooke Maczum, Jamie's wife for God's sake, telling her all of her secrets? Confessions from the past. Dreams of the future. For one thing, she and Brooke really aren't close friends, and another, Brooke is married to the one man she is never able to get out of her mind. Whether or not she's in love with Jamie is beside the point here. The fact is he *is* always on her mind and always in her life.

Is that it? Is she launching some kind of bizarre attack here? Steal Brooke's husband by endearing herself to her? Get Brooke to lay back and trust her and then swoop in and seduce him and take him? No. She's not even sure she wants him, but she knows she'd never do that. She'd never break up Jamie's marriage, never hurt his kids that way.

So, what the hell? Why is she sitting at the table with Brooke, laughing at a story Brooke is telling about the night she and her best friend snuck into a senior party when they were just sophomores in high school? Even more curious, why did she just tell Brooke about the day she'd snuck out of ISS and left the school campus to drive to St. Louis and the trouble she'd been in when the school had found her missing and called her dad?

Must be something to do with her and Brooke not living in each other's pockets since childhood. Not knowing each other's deepest, darkest secrets. Not seeing through the make-up, right through the skin to each other's flaws. Reaching forty and being alone, without a husband or children, is Lisa's greatest flaw. She wonders if Brooke feels that way. While she's sitting here talking to her, while Lisa is confiding in her, is Brooke sitting in judgment about the life decisions she's made?

Lisa takes a drink of her hot chocolate. No. She doesn't think Brooke sees her that way. She can't think that Brooke sees her that way, because she needs someone to stand aside and hold her hand from afar.

"Lisa?" Brooke clears her throat, the international sign for needing to say something uncomfortable. Lisa sits up, suddenly afraid of Brooke.

"What?"

"Are you ever going to tell Jamie? How you feel?"

Lisa feels the color drain from her face. "How I feel about what?" *What does that mean? Feel about—?* Her hands are clammy with sweat, but she keeps them wrapped around her mug and hopes that Brooke can't guess how uncomfortable she is right now. What normal woman would want another woman to confess to her husband that she's in love with him?

The thought is there and gone so quickly that Lisa sinks back in her chair, drained by the sudden onset of nerves. Play with fire, Lisa, she thinks.

"That you're unhappy. That you want more." Brooke sighs and reaches to touch Lisa's hand. "What you want. Why can't you trust him to know that you want your own family?"

Stomach still trying to settle around Brooke's words and the thoughts they brought to the surface, Lisa raises her eyebrows and shrugs. What if she does tell Jamie? All hell will break loose. Even if her friends didn't judge her and her lifestyle, all hell will break loose. If she tells Jamie, she will have to share with Angie and Makenna. And if Lisa tells them all she desperately wants her own family, that she wants very much to have a baby, then their whole friendship will suddenly focus on finding Lisa a husband and making Lisa her very own family. Nobody needs that kind of pressure. Besides, there are seven people in this friendship, and it's unfair for everyone to shift their attention to her. They've all got stuff going on; she's no more important than anyone else.

"He knows you've had something on your mind, Lisa," Brooke says gently. "He's worried about you."

"I don't know, Brooke." She rolls her shoulders and sits up straight again. Time to go home.

"When has Jamie ever judged you for something?"

Lisa opens her mouth to answer Brooke, but she says nothing. Because Jamie has never judged her. Never. He might scare away any man that shows any interest in her, but that's not judgment. That's concern. Friendship.

Isn't it?

"And for that matter, when have Angie and Makenna ever judged you?"

"Brooke."

"Besides that," Brooke goes on, "what's to judge? Even if you'd intentionally focused on a career and put family aside, what's wrong with that? A lot of women make that choice now. But none of us think you made a choice not to get married and not to have children."

"Well, then that really makes me pathetic, doesn't it?

I'm staring forty in the face, and I just can't find someone to love me?"

Brooke groans. "No. What it tells me is that you're waiting for the right person. There's no need to rush."

"Why does forty have to be such a big damned deal?" Lisa sighs and drags her fingers through her hair.

"It isn't. It's what you make it."

Lisa shrugs and raises her eyebrows. "Well, I guess I've made it a big damned deal."

"You're putting too much pressure on yourself."

"At the age of forty, a woman is much more likely to have a child with Downs Syndrome."

"There you go making that cup half-empty. At the age of forty, a woman is more likely to have twins."

Lisa laughs softly. "And that's a good thing?"

"Have you ever thought of adopting a baby?"

Wow. She's having this conversation. She walked right into this, and now she's sitting at her best friend's kitchen table with his wife, discussing adopting a child. It isn't that Brooke's not a good friend; she's become a good friend. No denying that. But Lisa would rather have this conversation with Jamie.

"You know." Lisa purses her lips and frowns at Brooke. "Jamie doesn't really judge me. He doesn't look at me and laugh and remind me of all the men through the years—"

"Lisa, it's not like you've dated the Dallas Cowboys football team."

"Well, no, I'm a little more discriminating than that."

They both laugh, and Lisa takes a drink of her hot chocolate, which has gone cold.

"Just listen, Brooke." She needs to say this. Because this

is the one thing that keeps her from confiding this new obsession to Jamie. And it *has* become an obsession.

Brooke nods.

"I've done some stupid things over the years, and yes, I know we all have. I've just had longer to do those stupid things, because I'm still single, and you guys have all settled down." She can see that Brooke wants to say something, but she's waiting for Lisa to finish. "But there are things that Jamie and I don't really agree on, and it comes out at work."

"What do you mean?"

"Teaching styles. Discipline. Classroom management."

"But that's okay. Not every teacher has the same classroom management."

"It is okay. You're right. But Jamie doesn't think so."

Brooke shakes her head. "I don't get it."

"It's not that we disagree. That's not a big deal. Of course, people disagree. Like you said, not every teacher has the same agenda or classroom management or whatever. It's what he says to me when he gets frustrated because he can't make his point to me."

"Make you see things his way," Brooke clarifies.

Lisa nods.

"What does he say?"

"That I would understand if I had kids."

Brooke drums her fingertips on the table.

"Like, the other day, I had a student come to me and tell me her sister came home drunk the other night. The sister is seventeen. My student was really upset. So we sat and talked through my free period. I don't have the answers. But I talked to her. No, no, I didn't, actually. I listened. When I mentioned it to Jamie later that day, he went off on me."

Brooke gives her a small nod, as if telling her to go on.

"That was my opportunity to lecture my student on the dangers of drinking. On the consequences of underage drinking. My opportunity to put the fear of God and the law in her. And if I had my own children, then I'd have known that. I'd have seen the opportunity to parent, rather than be a friend to my student. Parents aren't friends. They're parents."

"Well, I apologize for my husband being an ass about that," Brooke tells her. "It's just the way he is."

"I know that, Brooke. Believe me, I know that. And that's why I can't begin to think of telling him what's going on with me. I'm not suitable parent material. Not in Jamie's eyes. And I never will be, because I lack parenting experience."

"Why are you giving him so much power over you?"

"I'm not," Lisa answers quietly. "I'm not letting Jamie stop me from what I want. There's a lot of other stuff stopping me from getting what I want. Like no husband, for starters. But this is why I don't want to tell him."

"Which leads me back to my question. Have you ever thought about adoption?"

"I have, but I don't think it's a good idea. For one thing, why adopt a baby into a single parent home? Is that any better than the home it may have lived in, if its mother had kept it?"

"Of course, it is, if the mother was sixteen and scared and still in school."

"And this is ridiculous," Lisa ignores Brooke's

comment, "but if I have a child, I want to carry that baby. Give birth to that baby. I guess I want it all."

Brooke shrugs and nods. "So what? You're a woman. You're entitled to want it all. Go out and grab it for yourself."

"I'll just stop at the gas station on the way home and have the guy at the counter fill me up. Maybe in nine months I'll have something to show for it."

Brooke doesn't have the chance to acknowledge Lisa's sarcasm, because Jamie appears in the kitchen. He seems distracted, but he offers Lisa a smile.

"Hey. I didn't know you were still here." He touches her shoulder as he passes the table and opens a cabinet for a glass. "Did you say you need gas? It's really cold out there. Want me to go fill your car up for you?"

Lisa glances at Brooke and rolls her eyes. She shouldn't. She should be grateful he didn't hear and process the whole sentence.

"No." She takes another drink of her hot chocolate and tries to hide her distaste. Cold chocolate milk is one thing. Cold hot chocolate is quite another. "I need to get going, Brooke."

Brooke nods, but Lisa sees the wheels turning. She wonders what sort of kindling she's just set fire to.

"Is that an option?" Brooke asks quietly.

Lisa stares at her and waits for her to explain, because she's pretty sure Brooke isn't suggesting she do the long-haired guy at the gas station in hopes of making a baby with him.

Jamie fills his glass with ice water, tells them good night, and disappears back to whatever it was he was doing.

"A sperm donor?" It finally dawns on Lisa what Brooke is asking. Sure, it's an option. But not for her. She can't imagine a baby coming from a clinical situation involving a doctor and a stranger's sperm.

"I want it all," she repeats. "I want to make a baby with someone I love, someone who loves me."

Brooke nods. Lisa thinks she understands, but just in case, she lifts a hand to stop any other comment Brooke might make.

"And please don't suggest Jack. Because I'm not sure. I'm not sure about anything right now."

"I get it," Brooke whispers. "But, Lisa?"

"Hmm?" Lisa looks up as she puts her coat on. She reaches into her pockets for her gloves.

"Can I tell Jamie? Just to let him know what's going on? I'll ask him not to say anything to you. I just hate to see him so worried about you and so bothered by the fact that you aren't talking to him about something."

Lisa sighs and wonders for a moment if she's putting a strain on their marriage. If she's ever put a strain on their marriage. If Jamie's ever thought about taking her to bed and making love to her. If it's wrong that she's thought about it from time to time.

Lisa doesn't want to be responsible for putting any kind of strain on Brooke and Jamie's marriage. It's not likely that Jamie's pining for her, so that doesn't really concern her. But she doesn't want to think that Jamie is upset that she's suddenly talking to Brooke instead of him.

"Sure."

13

Angie

ANGIE WATCHES MAKENNA PUT THE FINISHING TOUCH ON A present for Aidyn. She glances at the tree in her friend's living room and then looks back at the package on the table in front of Makenna. There are six presents under Makenna's tree right now, and probably a hundred yards of ribbon and at least nine bows.

Makenna is meticulous when she wraps presents, whether they are Christmas presents or birthday presents or even bachelorette party presents. It makes Angie feel like a slacker, not that the presents under her tree aren't pretty each year. But sometimes, when she's wrapping stuff, she's so tired and so frustrated, and she just hates what she's doing. If Makenna ever feels that way, it's never evident on her face. Concentration. Rhythm. Peace.

Even happiness. But no, Angie's never read frustration or irritation on Makenna's face while she does this stuff. Then again, that attention to detail is what makes Makenna so good with her clients.

Perfection. Makenna's always been somewhat of a perfectionist. Angie used to be that way when she was in school. But the older she gets, and for God's sake forty is not that damned old—she's so tired of hearing that—the more those sharp edges of her life, of her determination and focus fade. Like the way her sharp hip bones have become rounded and soft under too many pieces of pie and Snicker bars and lattes that have gathered through the years and stuck to her hips like they are made of glue.

"Need more coffee?" Makenna asks suddenly. She doesn't break the silence since there is Christmas music playing, but she breaks something quiet around them, because for the longest time they've been sitting together and not talking.

"No thanks," Angie says on a sigh.

"What's wrong?" Makenna looks up and studies Angie closely. "You look so sad, suddenly."

Not so suddenly, Angie thinks, but she's not sure she really wants to have this conversation. Do other friends share one hundred percent of themselves? Or is it normal to want to keep at least just a sliver of yourself your own? Makenna is her best friend. Lisa is her best friend. She loves them both so much, and they've given her so much through the years. But does that mean they need to know when she feels lost or sad or angry? *Every time* she feels lost or sad or angry? Sometimes she doesn't even let Brian know the extent of what she's feeling or thinking.

"Just tired," she says quietly, and she knows from the

look on Makenna's face that she doesn't believe her. But Makenna will let it go, just as Angie has let it go in the past when Makenna has assured her nothing's wrong, that she's just tired.

Makenna eyes the present and apparently approves of it, and Angie watches her carry it to the living room and squat down to put it under the tree. Kenny G's saxophone is playing in surround sound through Makenna's house, and while Angie usually loves all of Makenna's Christmas music collection and just loves to tease her about it, today it is getting to her. Making her feel worse.

She'd been late to work this morning, and Angie hates being late anywhere. It had been the start of a crappy day, and she'd had a run-in with a bank customer—granted, by phone—but still. Nothing like getting your ass chewed on when you already feel like scum.

Makenna and Dave's tree is pretty. Well, all of Makenna and Dave's trees are pretty. They put up several, but they are all varying sizes, and some of them don't really get decorated. For instance, each of their girls has a little fiber optic tree in her room, and there is a little shiny, sparkly red aluminum tree in the half-bath. But the main tree is tall and decorated in red and gold and green with white lights. No garland. No tinsel.

Angie agrees with Makenna. Tinsel is so yesterday and so gaudy, and she hasn't had tinsel in her house for almost seventeen years. But she kind of misses it. Her mom always put tinsel on their tree when she little. Except for the years when her mom flocked their trees white, and Angie thinks those trees were beautiful. She and her mom had sprayed that canned snow in all of the windows those years, too. The house had looked like a winter wonderland.

Her mom's house had always looked like a winter wonderland at Christmas time.

"Do you ever wonder what the point is?" Angie finally asks Makenna. She figures her friend will whip out another present to wrap, because it will not do to have an uneven number of presents under the tree with two children in the house. Angie knows this from personal experience. Piper and Zach check the tree every day, and if there is an uneven number, they fight. They're too damned old to act that way, but they do.

Makenna isn't going to wrap another present, though. Angie watches her begin to tidy up the table, piling tissue paper and scraps of wrapping paper to the side.

"What do you mean?" Makenna asks her. Angie wishes she wouldn't have said anything, because she doesn't want to explain how she feels, and here she is bordering on that huge precipice again. Jump or turn back?

"It's the same every year. Isn't it?" Angie nods toward the tree and prays that her friend doesn't think she's insulting her decorations. "Get it all out. Put it all up. Give the same presents to the same people and hear the same bullshit thank you and then drink a cup to some old acquaintances and then put it all away until we have the energy to do it all again."

"Absolutely, I feel that way, Angie," Makenna answers sincerely. "Every damned year."

"It doesn't show."

Makenna shrugs. "My kids are younger than yours. And this time of year, my business thrives on Christmas spirit." She collapses back into her chair and yawns. "Besides, I'm not there yet."

"What do you mean?"

"Too early in the season for me to feel that way." She closes her eyes and rests her head against the chair. "It'll get me soon enough."

"I just wish it could be the way it used to be," Angie says, and she knows she's gone too far. Because now they are going to discuss her mom and Angie's grief, and Angie's not sure she can do that today.

But Makenna just opens her eyes and nods and says, "I know."

When Makenna leaves to pick the girls up from school, Angie leaves for home. She'd arrived at work at seven ten this morning to work on a few problems with the bank software and some direct deposit files. It's not like she'll be docked for getting there at ten after, but it still irks her. She'd left around one o'clock, and she feels guilty about that, too. Normally she works from seven until four, so she feels like she's playing hooky now as she drives home when it's not quite three in the afternoon.

She sees six houses with outside lights on already, even though it's not even sort of dark out yet. Brian thinks she's a voyeur, because she likes to look in people's windows as she drives by. Not to see people doing bad things or to see people undressing or to see people, period. It's just that she's always been curious about other homes and what they look like and what sort of family things the people who live there do. That curiosity is even stronger during the holidays.

It fills her with a longing and a hope so intense when she sees a lit Christmas tree in a window when she drives by. Even before her mom died, so no, no shrink or priest or friend can tell her this is just a phase that will pass as time heals her heart's loss. This year, she'd started seeing lit and decorated trees in people's homes before Thanksgiving. She'd mentioned it to Brian, and typical of Brian who hadn't noticed it, he'd said *yeah, people seemed to be starting earlier these days* and ducked his nose right back into his book. She could understand if it was a thriller or a mystery or even just literary fiction, but it wasn't. It was some book on hedge funds written by some financial guru.

Stopped at a red light, Angie takes a deep breath and decides to take a page from Makenna's book. If you don't feel it, fake it. Hell, who knows? Angie thinks. Maybe I can even fake myself into wanting Christmas to be here.

She turns the stereo on, but she can't find any holiday stations on satellite radio yet. That figures. No Christmas CDs in the car yet. She fumbles with her iPod and when she's just two blocks from home, she finds Bing Crosby and listens to the first few lines of "The Holly and the Ivy" as she pulls into their three-car garage.

No one's home. Surprised, Angie hurries inside and decides she will wrap a present or two. She'd expected Piper to be home; her friend drives her home on the days when Brian can't make it in time to pick her up at school. Determined to feel a little holiday cheer, Angie ignores the nagging thought that Piper will be sixteen and driving herself to and from school in a matter of months, because that's a damned sure way to feel depressed.

She lets Gibbs out the back door and watches for a moment as the miniature dachshund goes hopping, like a rabbit, over the snow in the yard. He looks back at her as if to ask her how she could make him go out when it's so cold, but as if realizing there's no sympathy, he trots out further until the snow is up to his belly. Angie is amazed at the hundreds of little paw prints in the snow.

She snorts with laughter as she watches the dog venture further into the yard. He buries his nose in the snow and then lifts it and looks at her, a small white pile on the tip of his nose.

Gibbs, named after Andy Gibb whom Angie was madly in love with when she was all of six or seven—and the other BeeGee brothers (because they're music is awesome)—is her baby. She'd wanted to name him BeeGee or Maurice, but Brian had flipped and put his foot down and said no way was she going to name their dog after some girlish-looking dude who sang falsetto. Angie had corrected him, of course, because any self-respecting BeeGee fan knows it is Robyn who is girlish-looking and sings in falsetto. But they'd finally compromised and decided on Gibbs.

When Gibbs makes his way back gingerly over the snow and stands at the back door looking up at her through the glass, she opens the door and lets him in. He's shivering. Still in her slacks and ruby red sweater from work, Angie scoops him up and goes to get a towel to dry him off and warm him up.

She carries him like a baby, and when he's dry, she gives him a treat and then goes to change her clothes. Ten minutes later, she is at the kitchen counter, sipping iced tea from a wine glass, listening to the soundtrack from the movie *Elf*, and wrapping a pair of jeans she got Piper. At first she thinks maybe she should have just poured herself a glass of wine, because maybe that would help her relax. But as she works on the present and listens to the music, particularly "Pennies from Heaven," she finds herself smiling and moving to the music. Too bad there aren't sugar cookies in the oven, she thinks, but then she remembers how she'd had to dance to get these jeans on and decides maybe she doesn't need sugar cookies anyway.

But, she reminds herself as she puts shiny green ribbon on the silver, red and green package with little Santas on it, it's the holidays (well, it's December and that counts) so shouldn't she allow herself sugar cookies or peanut clusters or fudge? It's the same thing she tells herself every year, and that brings her back full circle to what she'd said at Makenna's house.

It's the same every year. It's the same. Every. Year.

Before she can give herself a mental shake and get over it, the back door opens, and Piper walks in. Head ducked down, she pulls her long navy scarf from around her neck and then drops her backpack down on the kitchen floor and finally looks up to see Angie watching her.

The smile she gives Angie lights up the room twice as bright as the Christmas tree does.

"Hi Mom!" She hurries around the kitchen counter and plants a kiss on Angie's cheek. "I didn't know you'd be home early."

"Hi Pipe." Angie puts her arm around Piper's shoulders and gives her a kiss.

"I'm starved. Lunch was so disgusting."

"What was it?"

"Salisbury steak and chunky potatoes."

"Chunky potatoes?" Angie echoes.

"Supposed to be mashed," Piper says as she ducks her

head into the refrigerator. "Can we make some of these?" She holds a package of Nestle Tollhouse Break Apart cookies up for Angie to see.

Angie's stomach growls, and she laughs. She decides it's a good thing she's already given herself permission to eat some sweet stuff.

"Yes."

"Good. Can I help wrap?" Piper asks as she opens the package of cookie dough and then turns to set the oven to preheat. Angie doesn't answer her right away. Makenna's kids may be younger, but Angie's kids are still kids at heart. That's what keeps Angie a kid at heart. Maybe sometimes she forgets that, but how can she feel anything other than pure happiness that she and Piper are going to bake a few cookies and wrap presents while they listen to Christmas music?

14

ngie

THE TEMPERATURE HAS DROPPED FROM TWENTY-SEVEN degrees to ten, and the icy wind steals inside her. Angie's teeth ache, and her throat burns. She wishes for the tenth time that they could have stayed home tonight. The headache that hovered just under her skin all day has exploded. She'd managed to hold onto the Christmas spirit Makenna had shamed her into for a week, but now she's back to square one and irritated, a little depressed and tired, and maybe getting a cold on top of it. Piper hovers at her elbow, grumbling with every step.

"Zach!" Angie calls to her son. He is half-running and half-skipping toward the church. The parking lot and sidewalks are still covered in ice and snow, and Angie cringes, watching and waiting for him to slip and fall. Last year, he'd finished the second quarter of the school year in a cast. At least it had been his right hand. Brian had decided it was fate, since Zach is the only lefty in the family.

"Let 'im fall, Mom," Piper mumbles.

"Piper!" Angie snaps and looks over her shoulder. Her daughter is trailing several steps behind her now. Shoulders hunched, head down, her long hair hides her face. "That's a really nice thing to say about your brother."

"Well, he'll learn his lesson sooner or later, won't he?" Piper lifts her head now and cocks an eyebrow in askance at Angie. "Maybe not," Piper adds, as if she is just remembering that he broke his wrist last year.

"Get up here." Angie stops walking long enough for Piper to catch up to her again. "You're going to break your neck in those heels."

"Mom."

Angie doesn't have to look at Piper to know she's rolling her eyes at her. This isn't worth it. Nothing is worth this much trouble, and Zach's school program definitely isn't worth *half* this much trouble. Angie wonders again why she isn't one of those moms who lets her kids skip the program because they don't like to sing. Because singing is stupid. Because the music teacher is mean. Because the songs they have to sing are dumb. God knows, she'd heard every gripe in the book from Piper, when she was in grade school, and now she hears it all from Zach.

Piper slips her hand in the crook of Angie's arm. They huddle close and make slow but steady progress down the sidewalk. Angie catches herself thinking it would be nice if the church would pay to have the parking lot and sidewalks cleared. She really hates this uncharitable side of herself, and she should try to tamp that mean little voice down.

Instead, she focuses on the fact that she is curled in close to her daughter, and they giggle together a bit as they walk. At fifteen, Piper is rarely in the mood to have fun with Angie anymore, especially when they are out in public. She is a long-legged, blue-eyed beauty. Her two best friends are just as beautiful, and Angie often finds herself remembering her own high school years with her closest friends when she looks at Piper.

"Man, I have a headache that won't quit." Angie grits her teeth, but the words slip out anyway. She smiles and waves at other parents as they climb the steps in front of Queen of Peace Catholic Church.

"Why didn't we just stay home then?" Piper whispers.

"Zach." Angie breaks away from Piper and hurries up the steps to catch Zach before he disappears down the aisle of the church. Even this bugs her. Doesn't seem like that many years ago that he would've hung on her arm as they walked in and rattled nonstop about what songs they would sing and then rushed down the aisle, dragging her along, to find his class.

Zach tugs his coat off and turns and throws it at Angie. He flashes a grin that will break hearts one day and rushes down the aisle. Angie catches his coat and then turns back to see if Piper and Brian are coming. They are just stepping through the door, Brian with his arm slung around Piper's shoulders. Piper's cheeks are rosy red. Her eyes shine. Angie can't hear her, but she imagines she is laughing and telling Brian to leave her alone.

The church is already filled. Yet another thing that

annoys Angie. Some people must come over here at three fifteen, after they pick their kids up, and stake their claim on pews. Piper was in the Christmas program from kindergarten through eighth grade, and Zach is in the program now, and Angie and Brian have never sat in the front half of the church. Instead, they sit in the back section, the same area they sit in for Sunday mass, although then it's by choice. When Zach's class sings, Brian lugs the camera up to the front of the church to take the obligatory pictures. A couple of times through the years, Brian worked late and missed the program, and Angie had to do the pictures. The walk up the aisle and the squatting down to take the pictures—God forbid they stand in the way of those overzealous people who get their pews at three fifteen for just a few seconds to take a few pictures—is enough to wear her out. The older she gets, the harder it is to kneel or squat down, and even worse is the getting back up. Angie figures her bones pop loud enough that she sounds like the walking-rhythm section for the program.

Makenna waves at her from their pew. Seems like every year they are in the very same pew in the back part of church. At least they get the inner part of the pew, so they don't have to worry about seeing around the stone pillars.

Angie nods and says hello to other moms as she makes her way to Makenna and Dave's pew. Makenna looks cute and comfortable in jeans and a Rudolph sweatshirt. Angie suddenly feels uncomfortable and overdressed in her winter white slacks and shimmery red Christmas sweater. She hates this. Every year is a Russian Roulette on what to wear, and Angie always feels like she gets it wrong.

"Hey." Makenna stands and hugs her. "You look gorgeous."

Leave it to Makenna to say the right thing. Angie smiles and thanks her. She leans around her friend and says hi to Dave.

"Where's Piper?" Makenna asks as Angie asks if Lisa is there yet. Angie answers her own question; no one is sitting in the pew but Dave.

"Hi, Makenna."

Angie sits down and twists a bit so Piper can step by her. She watches as Piper leans into Makenna's hug. Piper's smile still lights up her face, but her face is that of a teenager now, not that sweet little girl Angie used to rock to sleep at night. The hollows just under her cheekbones and the eyeliner and shadow on her eyes are strikingly beautiful, but looking too closely makes Angie sad. Seems like Piper should still be only three or four, and Angie spends a lot of time these days looking at her daughter and wondering where those years went.

"Lisa coming tonight?" Brian asks as he sits down beside Angie. She hands him Zach's coat, distracted as she looks around to see who is here. Brooke, two pews in front of them, catches her eye and waves.

"Hi, Brooke." Angie leans forward and scoots a bit to her right, so she can talk to Brooke around the people in front of her.

"Seems like we were just here, doesn't it?" Brooke asks her. She smiles and raises her eyebrows.

"I know."

"Lisa called a few minutes ago. She's on her way."

"Good!" Angie turns to Brian to see if he heard Brooke.

"Is she sitting with us or with the Maczums?"

"I dunno." Angie shrugs. She looks around and takes the moment to calm herself. Yes, she'd dreaded this moment all day, but why? Really, what is the big deal about coming to the school program? Zach didn't have homework. Piper has a test to study for, but Piper never cracks a book until nine or later anyway.

Suddenly the program is starting. The second graders are the show-openers tonight. They file into position on the altar, all of them dressed in green tops and black pants. Angie smiles; the little kids are all so cute. They're all so excited to be here, to sing for everyone. When Zach had been in second grade, they had sung songs about the nativity. Angie sinks her teeth into her lip. What about Piper? What had her class sung in second grade? Or sixth grade? Or first grade?

Angie glances at Piper, her stomach clenching when she can't remember anything Piper's classes did in the program. What kind of mom doesn't remember this stuff? Isn't it really important stuff to remember?

As the kids finish "O Christmas Tree," Angie sees Lisa slip into the pew next to Brooke. She smiles and waves when Lisa glances back at her, but she wonders what's going on in Lisa's mind these days. She still hasn't heard any details about her trip to Champagne with Jack. Okay, so she doesn't want or need *those kinds* of details, but still. Lisa is her friend, and she went out of town with a man for a holiday. It bears discussion.

Aidyn is in first grade. Angie shrinks back in the pew as Makenna slips past her to walk the aisle and get pictures of her as the first graders step up, front and center. They are all dressed in their Sunday best, though

Angie has to laugh at that. Sunday best these days seems to mean anything from dresses and tights to blue jeans and T-shirts.

"Mom, Aidyn's so cute!" Piper gushes as she leans toward Angie. Angie puts her arm around Piper, but she keeps her eyes straight ahead on Makenna's daughter. The first graders are singing "Rudolph the Red-Nosed Reindeer," which is cute, because when Aidyn was little she was scared to death of Santa's reindeer.

It comes to Angie then. Piper's class sang "Frosty the Snowman" in kindergarten. They all wore white sweat suits with black hats and orange paint on their noses. First grade was "Santa Claus is Coming to Town." Second grade they sang "The First Noel," but Piper had left school early with the flu that day. Third grade they sang "Joy to the World."

"Aidyn's croonin'," Brian says with a laugh. Aidyn has overcome her fear of the reindeer, and she thinks she is a junior *American Idol*. She is clearly giving her performance her all. Angie laughs quietly.

Fourth grade was "Winter Wonderland," fifth grade was "O Holy Night."

Angie looks at Piper and twists in the pew again as Makenna comes back to sit down. Piper looks back at her, *really* looks at her, and smiles.

Zach's class sings "Toyland." Honestly, the sixth graders sound terrible. Since second grade, Zach's class has sounded terrible. Just like every other class once the kids start getting older. Some of them get self-conscious and just won't sing, and some of them get loud and stupid. To Angie, that's worse. But seriously, "Toyland"? How does "Toyland" work with any group of kids who don't want to be up in front of a crowd of people singing? At least give them "Jingle Bells," so they have something upbeat to work with, and save "Toyland" for a special choir or something.

Angie squirms in the pew and wonders if anyone else feels as uncomfortable as she does. This is ridiculous. It sounds like a funeral dirge. It only gets worse, when the eighth graders sing. Their song is "Gesu Bambino," which Angie knows and thinks is a beautiful song. But not by a group of kids who would rather be at home on Facebook or playing *Call of Duty*. She's pretty sure that Zach didn't sing with his class, and now she looks for Jamie's son, Daniel, to see if he is singing.

As bad as it is, as painful as it is to sit and listen to this, Angie still usually finds herself near tears. Every year she starts out hating this night and fighting a bad mood and then every year, after the kids start singing and she's sitting in the pew with Piper and Brian and Makenna and Dave, and sometimes Lisa, Brooke and Jamie, she's overwhelmed by the music and the songs and the feeling of family. Maybe it's the way the songs take her back like a time machine that zaps her back through the past. Back through the years when her kids were little. Through the years when she was a kid at home. She gets all weepy, like she's at her child's wedding instead of the Queen of Peace School Christmas program.

Tonight she's not moved to tears. The kids, other than the little ones, sound so bad it really bothers her. When each individual class is finished, the whole school comes together to sing two songs. Tonight they sing "Silent Night" and then "Joy to the World," and there are kids who aren't singing and there are older kids who are singing so loud, it sounds like they are screaming. Instead of feeling cozy and wrapped in memories and happy sad, or as Piper sometimes says, sappy, Angie is angry. Offended, even. Where in the hell is the music teacher? Why are they letting these kids get away with this? It's a Catholic school, performing a Christmas program in their Catholic church, and it sounds so disrespectful it makes Angie's head hurt worse. When the program is over an hour and a half later, Angie finds herself thinking of all the things she could have gotten done at home instead of sitting here feeling angry and disgusted. That certainly doesn't bode well for the holiday season. Well, Angie thinks, that's just stupid. How she feels about this program has no bearing at all on her holiday. And yet, she feels a little robbed of that experience: being moved to tears at least once by the music tonight.

She nods when Makenna and Dave ask if they are meeting at Mort's for dinner. She keeps her eyes toward the front of the church and watches for Zach. He hurries down the main aisle, following closely behind Aidyn, Ariel, and Jamie's boys .

"Meetcha there," Lisa calls and follows Brooke and Jamie to another exit.

As Zach shrugs into his coat, he tells Brian something, but Angie can only catch bits and pieces. He's mad about a couple of older boys acting stupid while they were singing the closing songs. Angie prays that Zach will never be so disrespectful. She and Piper follow the guys out of the church and back across the slick parking lot. She realizes she is frowning, and her head still hurts, and she takes a deep breath and tells herself to relax.

"That sucked," Piper says as they get to their shiny

silver Sequoia. Brian's vehicle. Angie loves riding in it, but she feels like she's driving a city bus when she's in the driver's seat.

"It did suck," Angie agrees. "Worse than usual."

"Let him skip it next year."

Angie looks over her shoulder at Piper and smiles. Of course, she's not going to let Zach skip the program next year. Maybe it sucks, but it's a tradition. They suffer through the program that is at least forty-five minutes longer than it needs to be, and then they all go to Mort's for dinner.

It's always the same. Year after year.

"No way," Angie tells Piper. "You don't change tradition."

15

M akenna

MORT'S IS BILLED AS A BAR AND GRILL, BUT ALL PRETENSES aside, it's a tavern. Complete with a scarred wooden floor, cold beer on tap, and a few hard-ass looking waitresses, Mort's serves greasy food. Cheeseburgers, onion rings, fried chicken—you name it, Mort's serves it.

They come here every year after the school program. In fact, they are here often enough that the waitresses know them by name if not by their regular order, and other friends often "remember" their rehearsal dinners being held here.

Makenna orders a bottled beer and a cheeseburger. She doesn't eat much meat, but she loves cheeseburgers. Ariel and Dave share an order of fried chicken, and Aidyn eats chicken strips. Makenna watches with a smile on her face as Angie studies the menu. It's as much a routine as coming to the bar, as if Angie expects the menu to change from time to time, or maybe she's just looking and hoping something new will jump out at her. Tonight Angie orders hot roast beef and mashed potatoes on bread, smothered in gravy. When she sees Makenna watching her, she grins and shrugs in defeat.

"What's another few pounds?" Angie mumbles.

"Another year, another few pounds." Makenna laughs and nods. "By the time we die, we'll be blimps."

"That's a nice thought."

Piper sips a diet soda and rolls her eyes at Angie and Makenna. There is no jukebox at Mort's, just a TV hanging in the corner above the bar. They don't need background music, though. The conversation among them always buzzes, and the continuous lilt of the dialogue is soothing and comfortable.

Makenna looks up when she hears the door open across the room. Lisa walks in with an arm slung over Jared's shoulders. Lisa's smile is worn, a little rough at the edges, but her eyes are warm when she sees Makenna looking their way. Makenna is surprised Jared allows her to put her arm around him. Jared and Zach are both pretty prickly about any show of affection these days from their moms or any of their moms' friends.

"Hey." Makenna stands as Lisa makes her way across the tavern. Makenna hugs her, and because Lisa's smile does seem a bit worn, Makenna takes a chance and gives her an extra squeeze and a pat on the back. She and Angie still haven't had a chance to catch up with Lisa, to hear about the trip to Champagne. Actually, Makenna had kind of hoped Lisa would bring Jack tonight, but maybe that's pushing it. Not like she would know how serious things are between Lisa and Jack, since Lisa's not talking.

"It's cold out there," Lisa groans and shivers inside her black leather coat. She tugs off her gloves and stuffs them in her coat pockets before she shrugs out of her sleeves and drapes the coat over the chair by Makenna.

Makenna presses her lips together to keep from saying anything about how Lisa wouldn't have to come to the program if she didn't want to. That's not true, though. Lisa has been right beside her and Angie every step of the way through motherhood, and Makenna knows everyone here would miss her if she decided to do something else on the night of the school Christmas program.

Kind of the way everyone missed her over Thanksgiving. Makenna thinks she could deal with Lisa making some changes, if it means that she's seriously involved with someone. If Lisa's in love with Jack, then yes, maybe some of their dynamics will have to change. But seeing Lisa happy would make those changes worth it.

"Did that program suck or what?" Jamie asks as a big gust of wind blows in behind him and Brooke. "I think it gets worse every year."

"Don't get me started," Angie mumbles. Makenna takes a healthy drink of her beer and nods when Angie looks at her.

"Half those kids don't want to be there," Makenna says as she tucks her hair behind her ear. "And then you saddle a class with that kind of want-to with a song like "Toyland'?"

"What was that song your class sang, Daniel?" Jamie asks. He nods when the waitress approaches, because he wants a beer and she knows it. "I've never even heard of it."

"I don't know," Daniel mumbles and shrugs. He asks for a soda and then stares at his plate. Makenna knows he didn't sing; she's pretty sure she hasn't heard ten words come out of his mouth for the past year. But she also knows without a doubt that Daniel wasn't one of the kids being obnoxious and yelling up in front of the church.

"I know the song," Angie announces. "We had it on a record album. It's a pretty song, but not really for a bunch of kids who have no interest in being there."

"Someone should suggest a choir," Dave says as he takes a long drink from his bottled beer. "You know, just round up the kids who want to be there singing. Maybe the kids that have some talent, and go from there."

Makenna agrees, but she feels like they've beaten this dead horse into the ground, so she inches closer to Lisa.

"How's it going, stranger?"

"Good," Lisa answers. "Just so much going on. I'm so tired, and I know if I blink, I'll miss something this time of year."

"I was hoping you would bring Jack. Ang and I wanna get to know him."

Lisa smiles wistfully. "I thought about inviting him. But I wasn't sure."

Wasn't sure, Makenna thinks. About what? About bringing him into our circle and maybe what all of us would think about that? Or does Lisa mean she's not sure about Jack?

"How was Thanksgiving?"

Lisa's grin leaves no room for doubt. She's not unsure about Jack. More likely, she's unsure about how he would be welcomed into the fold. Translation: she's unsure about Jamie and how he would treat Jack.

"It was fun." Lisa's warm, butterscotch voice fills with affection. "Kind of scary meeting his family, but it was really good."

And apparently that's all Makenna is going to learn about Thanksgiving and Jack, because Piper sits on the other side of Lisa and tugs at Lisa's other arm.

Makenna looks around the table at everyone talking and wonders if anyone's really listening and as much as she loves them all, she's ready to go home. She'd noticed this peculiar feeling the first time a couple of years ago. Sure, it's fun to be together, but sometimes it feels like they're here, together, because they're supposed to be here. They're talking and laughing by rote memory, and maybe this time doesn't measure up to last year or the year before, and Makenna yearns to be at home, tucked in the recliner by the fireplace with a book in hand.

She wonders if someone walking by outside sees their group and wishes he or she could join them. It's cold outside, and there're cheesy cardboard cutouts of Santa and Christmas trees in the windows. Makenna imagines some kind of Christmas music playing, something like "Christmas Island," and someone outside looking in, and she wonders if they look cozy and happy the way people do in the movies.

The funny thing is, and she knows this for a fact because it happens year after year, even though she doesn't feel fully present here right now, next year, she'll look back on this night and hold it as a special memory.

"Hey." Angie pulls her camera from her purse. She motions for Makenna, Lisa, and Piper to scoot closer together and the weird feeling, the wish to be at home passes, and when Makenna smiles, she means it.

Makenna and Lisa laugh when Angie snaps a quick picture of Zach and Jared talking at the end of the table. They're huddled together over Zach's PSP. Jared raises his head just enough to look at Angie, but Zach completely ignores her.

"No fair!" Piper calls when Angie turns to take a picture of Ariel and Aidyn. She jumps up from her chair and hurries to squat between the girls, and then suddenly three Hollywood smiles beam at Angie.

"Can't beat that one," Angie says with a smile. She drops her camera back into her purse and looks up just as Makenna gets a picture of her with her phone. "Oh, I'm sure that's lovely."

Makenna shrugs. "I should've waited until Judy brought your food." Judy is the waitress they have drawn tonight. "Just to show you ordered something different."

"You didn't order a burger?" Lisa's eyes go wide with surprise.

"Roast beef and mashed potatoes."

"Oh, that sounds good," Lisa answers with a nod. "I got a cheeseburger."

"Me, too."

"Live a little, girls. Step out of the box," Angie tells Makenna and Lisa.

"Maybe next year," Makenna answers and again she wonders about the scene they present to someone on the outside looking in.

16

J amie

JAMIE DOESN'T KNOW WHERE IT CAME FROM, BUT THE headache is making him mean. Actually, that's a lie. The headache is making him mean, no question, but he knows just exactly where it came from. He'd heard the music coming from the teacher's lounge before he'd opened the door. It wasn't particularly loud, but he did hear it. *That's* not it, though.

When he'd pushed the door open and stepped inside, he'd found Lisa and Jack dancing to "Pennies from Heaven." Not like dancing-dancing, body to body. Like something old fashioned and fun. Hell, he didn't know dances from tutus. Some kind of jitter-bug looking thing, maybe. And it's not like they were a hundred percent into it and heading off to audition for *Dancing with the Stars*.

But they were laughing, and even kidding around, they look good together, and they aren't bad dancers. Three other teachers were at the round lunch table watching them and laughing while they ate, and it just rubbed him the wrong way.

First of all, who the hell ever heard of dancing in school? Teachers dancing in school? During a school day? And the music? The hair on the back of his neck had stood at attention, and he'd kind of seen red, and instead of laughing with the rest of them, he'd muttered something angrily (he doesn't even know what) and moved to turn the radio down a bit.

Lisa hadn't even looked at him. Instead, she and Jack had left the lounge, heads together and laughing. Jamie had grabbed his lunch and a bottle of water from the refrigerator and returned to his classroom. He'd eaten lunch at his desk while grading papers, and he hadn't given Lisa and Jack much thought. Except for thinking how Lisa should watch what she's doing.

She's a single woman, and it doesn't do for a single woman to act like that with a man in the work environment. Jamie even considers talking to her about it, about how people who see her dancing with or huddled close, talking with Jack, are going to talk. Did he really need to tell her what they were going to be saying about her?

He'd started to. All afternoon, he'd pushed Lisa and what he'd seen in the lounge out of his mind. But then after school, he'd heard her walking down the hall. He'd known without looking that it was Lisa. Never mind that he knows the rhythm of her walk, or that he knows when she's wearing a dress shoe with a heel that makes a noise or tennis shoes or Ugg boots that don't make noise.

He'd called out to her, and then she'd stepped into his room, and he'd just kind of dumped it all out and told her he didn't think her behavior in the lounge was appropriate. She'd stared at him, clearly shocked by his words.

"Just stop." She'd raised a hand to stop him, and he'd stopped and right now, at this moment, he realizes he'd expected her to agree with him. To nod and say yes, he was right, and she really should watch what the hell she's doing, especially at work.

Jamie climbs up into the cab of his truck, still thinking about Lisa and Jack. The headache still hasn't quit. What the hell had he been thinking? Did he really think he was going to sit there and lecture Lisa, and she was going to take it? First of all, when had Lisa ever sat still for being told she was wrong?

Second, she wasn't wrong. She and Jack were having fun. There was obviously nothing inappropriate going on in the lounge, and it could just as well have been any other two teachers getting caught up in the fun of the season and spinning around the room for a minute.

Jamie turns the radio in the truck off. He's doing it again. Lisa is on the brink of a serious relationship, and he's doing his best to step in and break it up. Why? Why does he keep doing this to her? Is he jealous?

Hell yes, he's jealous, but there are about fifteen layers to that jealousy, and every one of them goes far deeper than her whiskey and sex voice and her ass in her painted-on jeans. Okay, maybe one of those layers doesn't quite go beyond the physical, because what man in his right friggin' mind can look at Lisa and not see how sexy she is?

He bites off an expletive as he pulls into the parking lot of the grocery store. It's never a good thing to do this, to think about Lisa Fairchild as anything other than his best friend. He sits for a minute after he turns the truck off. Can't walk into the market when his dick's on full salute. Can't take that home to Brooke, either. She'd had her insecurities about him and Lisa when they'd first been married, but she'd stopped worrying about it after she'd seen there was nothing more to them than friendship.

He's never laid a hand on Lisa, and mostly, he has no desire to. She's gorgeous, yes, but he thinks (and he's always kind of thought) that being involved with her would be a little like being with his sister. Besides, he's married. Happily married. He loves Brooke. If he didn't, he wouldn't have asked her to marry him all those years ago, and he wouldn't have had children with her.

Okay, so what the hell is he doing to Lisa? Safe now, he climbs out of the truck, slings the door shut, and clicks the locks. He pulls his cell phone from his pocket and calls home.

"Hey. I'm going to bring dinner home," he says when Brooke answers the phone.

"Oh. Okay." She sounds harried and out of breath.

"I'm at Sean Johnson's," he tells her. It's not a big store; in fact, it's more of a small neighborhood market. But he and Brooke stop here often for milk or bread or their homemade pizza that they make right in the back of the store.

"Pizza?" Brooke asks hopefully.

"Sound okay?"

"Yes," she groans and then she laughs. "I've been baking. And I'm wrapping a few presents. I was just wondering what to fix for dinner."

"See you in a few."

"Jamie, what's wrong?" she asks before he can hang up. How does she do it? She senses when he's upset or angry about something often before even he realizes it.

"Headache."

"Mm." That means she doesn't believe him. Or at the very least, she knows that there's more to it than a headache. How the hell is he going to explain this one to her?

How the hell can he explain it to himself? He walks through Sean Johnson's to the back counter. Martha, the little old woman at the counter, smiles at him and pats his hand when he leans in to talk to her. She asks if he wants the regular, and he says yes, and he thinks how simple this is. Ordering pizza from this woman as he's been doing for the past ten years, and he wishes everything could be so damned simple.

Okay, so what is for sure is that he's not in love with Lisa Fairchild. He's not in lust with her. Seeing a woman's beauty or sensuality or whatever the hell you want to call it doesn't mean anything. He's a man. Men notice pretty women. He cares about Lisa. Absolutely true. He's loved her from day one, when he'd ridden his bike down the street one spring day when he was fourteen and seen her shooting baskets at the house that had recently been sold.

She couldn't dunk, but damn, she had a gorgeous jump shot. He'd stopped at the end of her driveway, leaned a foot on the curb, and watched her swish eleven in a row before she'd noticed him. From the top of her driveway—

the house was on a hill—she'd stood with her hands on her hips and lit into him for just sitting there watching and challenged him to a game, and that was that.

Three nights later he'd told her every damned thing there was to know about Jamie Maczum. Sitting on the front porch of her house, which she hated, they'd spilled life stories and secrets and soda, and through the years, he'd never once regretted that his best friend was a girl.

He doesn't regret it now, that his best friend is a woman. He just wishes it could be simple. It should be simple.

So he's not in love or lust with her. He has the perfect life with Brooke and the boys.

He pays for the pizza and a twelve pack of beer and heads back out to his truck.

Okay, he thinks. No inappropriate feelings for Lisa. He doesn't want Lisa that way. So, why does he keep sabotaging her chances of a relationship? Of marriage and her own family?

Because even though he doesn't want her that way, he doesn't want anyone else to have her, either.

Jamie frowns as pain spikes between his eyes. That thought's bad enough, but something maybe a little more volatile, a little more dangerous occurs to him as he pulls into his driveway. The Christmas lights are on, and the house looks inviting. Brooke is inside baking. Pinwheel cookies, he bets, and maybe snickerdoodles.

If he admits to scaring away Lisa's boyfriends through the years because he doesn't want anyone else to have her, he has to wonder why the hell Lisa lets him do it time and time again.

17

Lisa

THE GREASE-SOAKED BROWN PAPER BAG ON THE COFFEE table is empty. Lisa and Angie are sprawled on opposite ends of the couch, and Makenna is curled up in the recliner. Angie drains her second beer and sets the bottle on the floor.

"Death by Mexican," Lisa says with a laugh. "Damn, that was good."

They'd planned a girls' night out, and though they rarely do it at Lisa's house, it seemed the place to be for the night. No husbands or kids to distract them or hinder conversation. No social constraints like fashion faux pas, so all of them are comfortable in sweats and running shoes. Angie's face, free of makeup, makes her look to be about twelve, and Makenna's hair in a ponytail, likewise, makes her look about thirty years younger.

Mort's not only does cheeseburgers and fries, but also Mexican food, which they find funny because Mort is certainly not Mexican. But then just about every restaurant you look into these days offers Mexican food, and Mort's is seriously the best in town.

"I didn't need that second beer," Makenna mumbles from the recliner. "I can't stay awake."

"Wake up," Angie tells her. "We're decorating the tree."

Lisa lifts her head from the arm of the couch and gives Angie the evil eye. "We're what?"

"Decorating your tree," Angie repeats. "It's the tenth of December, and you don't have a tree up."

"I'm aware of that," Lisa answers. "I'm fine with it."

"Not this again." Angie sighs.

Lisa doesn't want to put a tree up this year. Lisa doesn't want to put a tree up most years, and her friends guilt her into it. She has nothing against Christmas; in fact, she loves Christmas. But what she loves most about it is being with the people she loves, and that means she is always at Angie's, Makenna's, or Jamie's house. And so why does she need a tree in her house, where she is alone?

"Okay, okay," Lisa says on a groan. "We'll put my tree up. But, tonight?"

"Why not?" Angie stretches and then swings her legs to the side of the couch and sits up. "It'll be fun."

Makenna giggles from the recliner. "Remember that year we did my mom's basement tree for her? We were like fourteen or something."

"Sixteen," Lisa corrects her. "Because we had to leave and get more garland."

"Right." Makenna nods. "Because Angie was wearing Mom's silver garland like a boa, and she tripped on it and broke it."

"You don't break garland." Angie shakes her head and stands up.

"That was fun."

Lisa ignores the look Angie gives her and slowly sits up.

"We could put the tree up and maybe talk while we do it," Angie says as she eyeballs the corner of the living room. She stands with her hands on her hips, and she turns to study the spot in front of the window.

"What are you doing?"

"Deciding where we're putting your tree."

"It's my tree." Lisa stands up. She winces when her back pops. "It's my tree. I decide where it goes."

"Okay. Where's it go?" Angie asks.

"I don't know," Lisa answers and mimics Angie, studying potential spots for the tree. "I like it in the corner—"

"But then you can't see it through the front window." Makenna sits forward. Lisa nods, because she knows that's important to Makenna. She's always talking about driving down the street and looking in at people's Christmas trees and how it makes her feel all warm and fuzzy inside.

"Let's do the window," Lisa says. "We can move the TV to the corner."

Angie nods. "Let's get your stuff."

The three of them troop down to the basement.

"Lisa, when are you going to bring Jack around so we

can get to know him?" Angie asks as the three of them wrestle the Christmas tree box off the storage shelf.

"Possibly never," Lisa answers. They set the box on the floor, and Lisa rubs her hands together to wipe off the dust. She laughs softly when she sees that Angie and Makenna are frozen in place, staring at her.

"Why not?" Makenna asks softly. "Are you not seeing him anymore?"

"I am still seeing him." She tugs the box tops open and stares at the tree limbs. She hates this part. This was always her dad's job. Putting the tree together. Putting the lights on it. She only did the fun stuff, the actual ornaments. Angie and Makenna have help with this part, too. Brian and Dave help with the actual tree and the lights, and this is one reason why Lisa wouldn't mind skipping the whole Christmas tree ritual each year.

Except when Lisa looks up, she sees her two friends watching her closely, and she knows they are waiting for an explanation about Jack. But she sees more than that. She sees *her* support system. Through years and years of putting up lights and Christmas trees and health issues (from sore throats to an appendicitis attack when she was twenty-eight) and job searches and losing lovers. She raises her eyebrows as guilt threatens to drown her. How can she keep so much from Angie and Makenna? They love her. She knows they do. They won't judge her. They wouldn't judge her if she said she wanted to give up her teaching job and be a pole dancer.

Still, when it comes to slicing herself open and giving them everything, she's paralyzed.

"I mean." She sighs and takes the plunge and pulls out the first set of limbs. Angie and Makenna do the same, and then they follow her up the steps, "We aren't like… steady. Or maybe we are, but it's not like he asked me to *go steady*. Ya know? I mean, how do adults do that? What do we call it? We're too old for class rings. But I'm not dating anyone else, and I don't think he is."

Unless you count his ex-wife, she thinks. She knows that when she first started dating him, he was just coming off round two or three with the ex. Actually, she decides, that might *be* a red flag. Probably something she should be a bit more concerned about.

"So…" Angie shrugs. They work quickly on this part, getting the tree together, but they slow down when they start plugging in lights to make sure they all work. Because, inevitably, they don't. "What's he like?"

"Pretty incredible, really," Lisa answers without hesitation. She looks up from her spot on the floor, on her knees, and sees that the two of them are still watching her closely. They look like little kids, poking at a wounded bird, half-afraid they might hurt it, but more fascinated at what they see. "I don't want to bring him around, because…"

Lisa flops gently back to her butt and runs her fingers her through her hair.

"I don't want him around Jamie." She avoids their eyes, but she wonders what they're going to make of what she just admitted. She's aware that they could take her words and make them mean something entirely different.

"Because?" Angie prompts her. She grabs a butter dish full of replacement light bulbs from the end table and sits down on the floor by Lisa.

At least they are letting her talk, instead of jumping on the Lisa and Jamie bandwagon.

"Because he's run every man I've ever dated off one way or another."

"And you don't wanna lose Jack?" Makenna asks her. Angie's fingers move deftly from light to light, changing those that are burned out.

"No, I don't," Lisa answers simply. "I like him. I like him a lot."

"Are you in love with him?" Angie asks, never looking up from the lights.

"Maybe."

Angie lifts just her eyes to look at Lisa. "Really?"

"How do I know?" Lisa shrugs. "Right? Hasn't that always been my problem?"

"I don't think so," Angie answers. "I think you've always known you weren't in love. But something about Jack is different."

"Yeah." Lisa nods. "I don't know. There's still a lot I'm not sure about."

"But, maybe you're in love with Jack." Angie grins, but she's still concentrating on the lights.

"Jamie's being a dick about it," Lisa says, and she's thinking about the other day at school when he'd preached to her.

"What do you mean? You haven't brought Jack around any of us."

The last of the bad bulbs replaced, Lisa and Angie stand up, and the three of them begin winding the light strands around the tree. She bought it ten years ago. Sometimes Lisa thinks if she's going to go through the motions every year, she'd like a new tree. This one is skinny, and even when decorated, it looks a little pathetic. Wouldn't it be nice to have a big house like Makenna or

Angie and have a gorgeous, tall tree? Or a big, fat tree decorated with meaningful Hallmark ornaments or hand-made ones the kids did at school?

"Jack's a sub at school." Lisa still stares at the tree, but she's thinking about Christmas when she was seven, before her mom left. They'd made garland out of construction paper links, and at the time, her mom loved it, and Lisa hated it. Now she wishes she had someone to make garland with her. Her mom. Or a child. She's not picky. "He's not there every day, but he's around a lot."

"So Jamie's a dick to Jack at work?" Angie asks, and Lisa knows Angie is leading her to keep her talking.

"No, he's being a dick to me. I don't know if he's ever said jack to Jack."

"What'd he do?"

"He preached me a sermon the other day about inappropriate behavior in school."

"Do tell," Makenna says with a grin. "Were you and Jack making out in the coatroom?"

"Cloakroom," Angie corrects her. "When we were kids, it was the cloakroom."

"There aren't any cloakrooms at the junior high," Lisa answers. "The kids have lockers."

"So, you and Jack were making out in the locker room? What?" Angie laughs.

"No. We were dancing. Just being stupid. He was in the teacher's lounge. Finishing his lunch when I walked in. There were other people in there. The radio was on, and some old-fashioned kind of song was playing. I don't even remember what it was. But we were all joking about the music, and it was just one of those special moments that you know is gonna come back year after year and make you feel good."

"Like when we decorated Makenna's mom's tree."

"Like almost anything we do together," Lisa says with a shrug. "Jamie walked in. He was pissed. Because I was dancing with Jack. There was enough room to fit two people between us. Not that I should have to explain myself, ya know? I'm an adult. There's nothing between me and Jamie. Do you know what I mean?"

"Who's he to comment on anything you do?"

"Exactly!" Lisa says to Angie.

"So, what'd he say?"

"Nothing, then. He just marched over to the radio and turned it down. It was like he was my dad, and he caught me and Jack going at it or something. Jack and I just walked out together, didn't say a word."

"I bet that got him." Makenna can't hide the smirk on her face.

"Apparently, because after school that day, he caught me as I was passing his room. He informed me that my behavior at school was questionable, and did I really want to put that sort of image out there for my colleagues to see?"

"He's jealous," Angie says simply.

Lisa nods. Of course, he's jealous. He's been doing this crap to her since they've been friends. But he'd never made any move on her himself, back when they were both free to be together if they'd wanted to, and he sure as hell can't do anything now.

"Why's that fair?" Lisa blinks when her eyes suddenly fill. "Why is it fair that he can mess with me like this?"

"He can't have you, Lisa," Angie tells her. "But he doesn't want anyone else to have you, either."

"He could have." Lisa's voice is thick. She swallows hard and takes a deep breath. No crying. For God's sake, no crying. She hasn't done this in years. Not about Jamie Maczum, anyway. "He could have had everything, but he didn't want it."

"Oh, honey." Angie steps in and puts her arms around Lisa. "I know. I know."

Lisa allows herself a minute to cry on Angie's shoulder, and then she pulls herself together and stands up straight. "I hate the way it always goes, Ang. I can't have him. I know that. I love him too much to ever step in and hurt his marriage. I love Brooke and the boys. Why can't he let me go?"

"Does Jack know about Jamie?"

Lisa turns to look at Makenna. She rubs her fingers under her eyes, knowing her eyeliner has smeared with the tears.

"He knows that Jamie and I are good friends. But, no. He doesn't know there's more to it."

"Is there more to it?" Angie asks her gently.

"No." Lisa sighs. "C'mon, guys. I've told you a hundred times. Jamie and I have never been together. He's never even kissed me."

"What did you say? When Jamie said that to you the other day?"

"Just told him to stop talking. Haven't talked to him since."

"Did Jack say anything? About how Jamie acted in the lounge?"

"No."

Quiet surrounds them as they work on the tree.

"We need some Christmas music," Makenna says. "Got any?"

"Yeah. In the cabinet under the TV."

Makenna squats down and opens the cabinet to look.

"So what did you guys do over Thanksgiving?"

Lisa hesitates, a red and silver ornament in hand, and turns to look at Angie. "Just…we just hung out. His sister cooked everything. Dinner was delicious. We hung out by the fire. Went shopping the day after—"

"Really?" Makenna sounds delighted at the thought.

"Yeah. I mean, we didn't roll out of bed in the dark with all the crazies—"

"Hey!" Makenna frowns.

"You did?" Lisa laughs. "Sorry. But we went shopping, and we went to lunch. Had dinner with his sister again that night. Saturday, we went to his niece's basketball game. Hung out with his sister and her family. And then he and I went out Saturday night."

"For dinner?"

"Yeah, we had dinner. But we went dancing, too."

"Seriously?"

"We had a blast, guys," Lisa says honestly. "He's a great dancer."

"Seriously?" Makenna repeats.

"Started out very gentlemanly, but we ended up in a dark corner of a dance floor doing the grind."

"Scandalous for a junior high English teacher," Angie mumbles.

"Jamie would have dropped dead of a heart attack if he'd seen us." Lisa nods.

"And so I assume you continued the grind back at your hotel?" Makenna raises her eyebrows.

"Oh, God," Lisa growls and laughs at the same time. "Oh, man."

"I am so jealous," Angie says to Makenna.

"Okay, so he's good-looking, and he's fun. He's nice. You like his family. He likes to shop. He's a good dancer, and he's hot in the sack."

"Pretty much so, yeah." Lisa nods again.

"That changes after the wedding," Makenna says on a sigh.

"What part?" Lisa asks. She and Makenna watch Angie, who is the tallest of them, place ornaments in the highest part of the tree.

"All of it," Angie answers quickly.

The three of them laugh, and they step back to check their decorating job.

"Not bad," Lisa says softly.

"Not bad, really?" Angie turns to Lisa with a frown. "This tree kicks ass."

"Your trees kick ass," Lisa corrects her, and it is the closest she's ever really come to comparing their lives out loud for them to hear, and she wonders if she's just opened another can of creepy crawlies. But neither of them seems to hear the emotion in her words. Strange, because Lisa's all over the venom in her voice, and she knows something has to give soon or all hell is going to break loose.

If all hell breaks loose, it's all going to settle back into place with Lisa moving on and leaving the rest of them to their family lives.

"Are you kidding me?" Angie shakes her head. "This tree is the best this year. Do you know why?"

"Why?" Lisa cocks her head and waits for Angie to go on.

"Because we did it. Together. Just the three of us. No kids. No men. Just the three of us."

Lisa feels the burn of pent-up emotion in her throat. She nods. "Yeah. You're right."

"It's been too damned long since we've done this kind of stuff, girls," Angie says.

The song changes to "Have Yourself a Merry Little Christmas," and Lisa sees Angie's eyes fill. Lisa knows that even though this moment is theirs, Angie is thinking of her mom. Lisa puts her arm around her, and then Makenna is there, and they stand and laugh and cry together.

18

J amie

It's Friday night, and Daniel and Jared are at the high school basketball game with friends. Jamie had planned to go, but Brooke had asked him not to, because they had some stuff to do. He'd assumed she wanted to finish Christmas shopping or something. He has no idea what she's bought so far, what she has stashed away, or even where she stashes the stuff she buys. It used to be she would just stick it in their closet, but the boys figured that out quickly. Most of the stuff the boys open, Jamie sees for the first time, too, on Christmas morning.

He wonders what exactly she plans to buy if she's enlisting his help. They just put up a new basketball backboard outside last year, so it can't be that. Daniel isn't ready to drive yet and won't be for years, so she doesn't have her eye on a car. Something she wants for herself, maybe? But, that's so unlike Brooke.

"Hey, do you wanna go get..." Jamie stops mid-sentence when he sees that Brooke is pouring wine into two glasses. The good glasses, not the short cheap ones. Brooke calls these the pretty ones.

"What?" She looks up at him as she replaces the bottle stopper. *White wine. Some kind of Chardonnay, maybe? Why?*

"I was gonna ask if you wanted to go grab some dinner before we go."

"Before we go where?" Brooke asks with a frown.

"I dunno," he says, and he shrugs. "I just thought you wanted to run errands or do some Christmas shopping or something."

"Oh." She sounds surprised by the possibility, so apparently it isn't what she had in mind. "Okay. But I want to talk to you about something first."

Jamie's heart thuds dangerously hard in his chest. He lifts his hand and brushes it over his left side, as if he can push that quick jab of pain away. *Jesus, Maczum. Are you having a heart attack because your wife wants to talk to you about something?*

But what could she want to talk about? Oh. What if she's pregnant? Is that possible? Of course it's possible. But...But. What if?

Jamie swallows hard and reaches for Brooke's hand. What if she's thinking about leaving? He's sensed that she's been restless lately. That whole thing with going back to work. Wanting to be useful. Needing to do something. What if she's unhappy, and she wants to leave?

"What's wrong?"

"Why don't you tell me?" she asks quietly.

Oh, God. This is it. She's unhappy, and she's going to ask him to name the reasons why and when he can't, she'll say that's the problem. They don't communicate, and he doesn't get her, and she's tired of it, and she's leaving.

"What do you mean?" He lets go of her hand and picks up one of the glasses.

She laughs when he takes a big gulp and stares at her, waiting for her to drop the bomb.

"What's going on in your head, Jamie? You've been horrible to talk to for the past week."

Oh, man. Is she going to drag Lisa into this? Surely, she won't. If he and Brooke have marital problems, and the hell of it is, he doesn't think they do, they have nothing at all to do with Lisa.

But don't they? Isn't she always here? Inside you?

Jamie shakes his head to clear that annoying inner voice. He's panicking. His chest hurts. *My God, Brooke's going to leave, and I'm having a heart attack. What's going to happen to the boys?*

"Nothing," he says, and he shakes his head. "Just stuff from work."

"Stuff with Lisa?"

Oh, shit. He groans. He can deny ever having touched her, because it never happened. Never. Not even when they were sixteen years old, and it could have been written off as two kids playing games. But, he can't deny that he loves her. Some place inside him, not a big place, but there's a place inside himself that loves Lisa Fairchild just exactly the same way he loves Brooke.

"Yeah." Jamie shrugs. He hopes he looks casual and unaffected and maybe a little hungry, so maybe they can just bluff their way through this conversation, and Brooke can forget about wanting a divorce, and they can just go on with life. "We just got into it the other day."

"Again."

He nods but says nothing. His palms are damp, and his heart still hurts. He can't lose Brooke. Brooke and the boys are his life.

"Have you ever noticed that you guys tend to bicker more when she's involved with someone?"

"No, we don't," he says, and he tells himself to stay calm. Not going to do him any good if he's too defensive. "I mean, I just want her to end up with the right man."

"She's not going to end up with the right man," Brooke tells him. "Not in your mind."

"Why do you say that?"

"Because no other man is you."

Jamie opens his mouth, but he says nothing. What is there to say to that? Brooke doesn't seem particularly upset, even though she's just said something huge about his relationship with Lisa. He doesn't really know exactly what she said, but he knows it was huge, and it's here now in the kitchen with them. Not quite like the elephant in the room. It's the elephant in the pink tutu and tiara, doing a belly-dance on the kitchen bar right between them.

"She can't have you, Jamie," Brooke says softly. "I know you care about her. I get that. But you have to let her go, because she can't have you."

"What...But I..." Jamie stares at Brooke for a moment and finally takes another big drink of wine.

"You're saying," Jamie starts and then stops to think for a minute, "you're saying that Lisa wants to be with..."

"No. I'm saying that for years you have sabotaged every relationship she has. Intentionally or not, I don't know. But you have run off every guy she's ever dated, and yes, some of them were definitely bad news. But the thing is, you have to let go. Honey, I know there's something huge between you two. It was there years before you and I met. But you're married. You're happy with me, aren't you? Aren't me and the boys enough for you?"

"Brooke, you and the boys are my life." His voice is tight with emotion.

"Then be fair to Lisa. Let her find this." Brooke touches his face. Her fingers skim over his lips. "Let her figure things out for herself."

Jamie sighs and wonders what the hell is going on. His kitchen has become the twilight zone, and his wife is either warning him off another woman because she's going to leave him or she's warning him off another woman at the other woman's request, and he doesn't know up from down right now.

"When Lisa is unattached, you're happier. You're more relaxed. You're easy-going and fun for everyone to be around. Because you've got it all then. You've got your wife and kids, and you've got Lisa, smothered in this friendship and too involved in your life and your kids' lives to want to have a family of her own."

"But…"

"But when Lisa is seriously involved with someone, you're angry. You're uptight. You take it out on everyone else, not just Lisa or whoever she's seeing. Until finally she gets tired of it or the guy decides Lisa's not worth your big brother antics and takes off."

"Lisa wants to have a family of her own?" Jamie finally

picks up a thread of conversation that has caught his attention.

"Yes, she does." Brooke nods.

"Really." He never would have thought that. She'd always struck him as a professional woman who didn't want to be tied down.

No, she hadn't. Years ago, she'd talked about wanting to be in love and wanting babies, and then year after year when it didn't happen, she'd pushed it so far down inside her that it was easy for him to pretend that part of her didn't exist. Easier for him to think she could be happy just being his sidekick. His best friend. Part of *his* life.

"She's a bundle of nerves right now, and you're not helping."

Jamie purses his lips, thinking about Lisa and then wondering how his wife knows what Lisa is thinking.

"Does she talk to you?"

And then suddenly he remembers the recent nights when he's come to the kitchen to find his wife and Lisa at the table, obviously deeply involved in conversation and suspiciously quiet while he's in the kitchen with them and the way the hum of conversation grows again when he leaves them alone.

"She does, doesn't she? She stopped confiding in me, and now she talks to you."

"You stopped listening, Jamie."

"What about Makenna and Ang?"

"She hasn't told them, either."

"So...what? She's outgrown all of us? Or she's..."

"She's afraid of all of you. Of what you would say."

"Afraid? Lisa's afraid of her three best friends?"

Brooke nods. She finally picks up her glass of wine and takes a sip.

"You all found someone. You're all married. Happily-married. You all have children. She wants all of that for herself. Mostly she wants a baby, and she's afraid of what you would think."

"Why?"

"Because you're so judgmental. Apparently you guys don't see eye to eye on kids. She said it's obvious in your teaching styles."

"But. That's life. People don't agree on things all the time. Why would she use me as an excuse to not have a baby?"

"She's not. But this is why she won't talk to you. She thinks you would tell her she'd be horrible at mother-hood, and she's never said so, but I think a lot of that stems from her mom walking out on her when she was younger. She's not having a baby because she's alone."

"Single women have babies all the time these days."

"Is that what you would think? If Lisa came to you and told you she was pregnant?"

"Okay, if she were eighteen, I'd be upset. And I'd tell her. But she's a grown woman. That's her decision."

"Really? You would support her?"

"Of course, I would. Brooke, I would support her in any decision she made. So, maybe we see things differ-ently, but that doesn't mean I respect her any less."

"Look, it's just that she wants to be able to talk to you. Like it used to be. But she's really afraid of your reaction."

Jamie nods. He no longer feels like he's having a heart attack. Brooke's not going anywhere. But maybe Lisa is.

Maybe she should. Maybe it's Lisa's turn to live.

He feels like he's going to throw up.

"Brooke, it's not that I want Lisa for myself." He groans and reaches for her hand. "It's not that I want that kind of relationship with her. Please tell me you understand that."

Brooke chews on her lower lip and stares at his wineglass, rather than look him in the eye.

"Then what is it?"

"What am I to her, if she falls in love with someone else? I mean I changed with her, when you and I got married. Sure, we still talk. And now and then, I might tell her something from our house. If Daniel gets in trouble at school or if you and I have a fight, maybe. But I don't feel that I can give that much of myself to her now. I belong to you."

"You don't want to lose her intimate friendship."

"Her friendship. Her trust."

"That's not fair, Jamie."

"I know."

"You should get to know Jack."

He does know Jack, but not well. Probably he's an okay guy, but Jamie's hated him on sight since Lisa went out with him the first time.

Because he wants to be the one to take care of Lisa.

"Is she in love with him?"

"I don't know." Brooke sighs and raises her eyebrows. "I don't think she knows. Some days I think she does love him. Some days I think she's trying to sell herself on him so she can grab the brass ring and get married and have babies."

Jamie drags his fingers through his hair and hunches his shoulders up. He feels as though he's just run a marathon.

Brooke finishes her wine and sets her glass on the counter by the sink. "Let's go get dinner."

Jamie shakes his head. "Nah. I don't wanna go anywhere."

"Oh. Okay." Brooke drums her fingers on the countertop. "I think we have a couple of frozen pizzas we could fix."

"C'mere." Jamie takes her hand and tugs her toward him. "I love you. Just you. You know that, don't you?"

Brooke moans quietly as Jamie drags his open mouth over her lips and her chin and down her neck. He needs her close, needs to feel her body pressed head to toe against his. He needs to fill her and remind her that she is the only woman he wants or needs.

"C'mon." He stands and staggers hand in hand with her to their bedroom, happy that the boys will be gone for a while.

ngie

ANGIE MAKES AN EXCEPTION AND DRIVES BRIAN'S CAR tonight. She has a full load. Makenna sits in the front with her, and Lisa sits in the middle back with Aidyn. Ariel and Piper and all three boys are crammed in the very back together. Christmas music plays in the car—the fun stuff —like "Mr. Heatmiser" from one of the kids' cartoons. Angie can't even remember which cartoon it is, but she bets Makenna would know.

There is a line of cars a mile long waiting to turn into the North Pole. No one seems to care, though. Even the boys seem to be having fun. In the rearview mirror, Angie sees Piper talking to Ariel. Her daughter's smile is radiant and infectious. Piper is so serious, and she's so uptight about school that Angie always feels a loosening in her chest when she sees her smiling and having fun.

"We should work this sometime," Makenna says and leans forward to see the lights of the North Pole.

"Are you insane?" Angie shakes her head. "Brian and I worked last year. The bank was a sponsor, so we did a shift. It was like two degrees outside and maybe five in the little outhouse."

"Outhouse." Aidyn giggles. "You didn't stand in an outhouse, Angie."

Angie laughs. "Well, it looks like an outhouse."

Aidyn wiggles in her seat, and Makenna turns to look at her. "Uh-uh. Not yet. You gotta stay in your seat until we turn in."

The North Pole is a two-mile long Christmas light display. It started out small just a few years ago, and suddenly corporate sponsorship jumped in and built it up to an incredible wonderland for kids. Aidyn desperately wants to climb up on Makenna's lap so she can see better, but Makenna has told her only once they'd turned off the main road could she move.

"Angie didn't stand in an outhouse, did she?" Aidyn asks Makenna.

"No. But it is a little building that looks like one."

"Mom, we shoulda got hot chocolate," Piper calls from the backseat.

"We should've," Angie agrees and then Lisa announces that they can stop on the way back to Angie's house.

"My treat," Lisa tells them.

"For ten people? That'd be like one paycheck for me."

Lisa reaches up to nudge Angie's shoulder. "Makes Christmas shopping easy. This'll cover everything."

"No!" Aidyn squeals.

"Aidyn," Makenna warns, glancing back again at Aidyn. But, Lisa laughs and shakes her head.

"I already have yours wrapped and under my tree at home," she tells Aidyn.

"Seriously?" Makenna asks Lisa. "You have presents under your tree?"

"I do. Three, so far."

"Is mine?" Jared leans forward to ask her.

"Jared Michael." Brooke takes a swipe at him from the very back of the SUV. "I may have drawn the straw for the cargo seat, but I can climb over and swat you."

"You'd have to catch me first," Jared says, obviously not concerned. Brooke and Lisa glance at each other and laugh.

"Not a problem, Jared."

"You didn't even want your tree up yet, and see? Now you have presents under it. I'm so impressed." Makenna nods.

"Jack helped me wrap them."

"He's all that and a bag of chips," Angie says approvingly.

"Mommy, why is Jack a bag of chips?" Aidyn asks. Lisa laughs. Angie inches the SUV closer to the North Pole entrance.

"Can we really get hot chocolate, Mom?" Piper asks. Angie decides Piper is probably freezing, because she's only wearing a lightweight leather jacket. She'd reached the age of leaving comfort behind for style a few years ago, and she'd never looked back.

"Yes, Pipe, but not on Lisa's dime."

"Cool!" Ariel grins, and Angie sees her knuckle Piper.

"Ang, this music sucks," Makenna says when an ancient recording of "I'll Be Home for Christmas" begins on the radio. They are listening to the North Pole station, and of course, Angie knows the music boss beside her would never approve.

"I am so glad you're only like this at Christmas time," Angie tells Makenna. "You're worse than a backseat driver. You're like a backseat DJ."

"Yeah, well, you need help." Makenna winks at her. "Obviously."

"That's cheap!" Angie argues. "It's a radio station, not like a CD."

"Because you don't have any Christmas CDs."

"Girls!" Lisa calls. "Chill."

"Let's just sing," Piper suggests. Angie looks in the rearview again, as she inches the SUV further along. They will be the next car to turn into the Pole. Angie notices that Aidyn looks ready to explode with excitement. She feels a pang and wishes for just a moment that Piper and Zach were still young enough to believe in Santa Claus, at least to question him rather than pretending to believe for Aidyn.

"Sing?" Angie says and looks back at Piper.

"Yeah. Like fa-la...well, you know."

Angie snorts with laughter.

"Oh, Gosh, don't let Mom get started," Zach mumbles in disgust, which only makes Angie laugh harder.

"I'm thinking Bailey's in my hot chocolate," Lisa says thoughtfully.

"Who's Bailey?" Aidyn asks, and Angie cracks up.

"Oh, no." Piper's voice.

Still laughing, Angie pulls further into the street where

the North Pole is set up. She puts her window down and takes the cash Makenna hands her and passes it to the guy at the window. It is six bucks for a carload, and the guy sort of leans in Angie's window and makes a comment about how they did a good job of packing, and that makes Angie laugh harder.

"Want me to drive?" Makenna asks.

"Shut up," Angie says around a deep breath.

"She's not done." Zach still sounds disgusted.

Suddenly, Piper and Ariel are singing "Rudolph" and slowly everyone joins in, even the boys. The crazy laughter slows inside Angie, and she kind of sings as she drives, but not really.

"Why aren't you singing?" Makenna asks.

"Are you kidding me? I'm driving, and I'm looking at Christmas lights. I think adding one more thing might be asking for it."

"Good point," Makenna agrees. Aidyn tosses her seatbelt aside and scrambles up to sit on Makenna's lap. Daniel lunges for the empty chair, and Jared turns to look at Brooke, still in the back.

"Want him to move, Mom?"

"No, it's actually kind of interesting to see all of this backwards," she answers without looking at him. "As long as I don't puke."

"You're puking?" Angie calls from the front. "'Cuz I can just open the tailgate. Won't have to clean anything then."

"What kind of chips is he, Lisa?" Aidyn asks, and Piper, Ariel, and Lisa are still singing, only now it's "Jingle Bells."

"This is one for the books," Angie says softly to

Makenna. Aidyn demands to know what books Angie means, but Makenna answers with a small smile.

The lights of the North Pole finally grab everyone's attention, and the only sounds are the murmurs about how pretty they are. Lisa makes a comment about feeling like she's high as they drive through a long tunnel of lights, and then Piper and Ariel start singing again.

They hit the drive-thru at Billy's Beans with orders for seven hot chocolates, two regular coffees, an iced-coffee, and a latte.

"Seriously? Who got an iced-coffee? It's like the Arctic outside."

Angie watches in the rearview to see who claims it. Piper takes a tiny sip of her hot chocolate. The iced-coffee goes to Daniel, and Angie watches in amazement as he takes a big drink.

"Dude. It's cold. What're you doing?"

He grins but says nothing.

Makenna drinks the latte. Angie and Lisa have the regular coffees, and Angie has every intention of adding some Bailey's to hers when they get back home. She knows Lisa will, too.

The guys are watching some action movie when they get back. Angie takes her coat off as someone fires some kind of automatic gun on the movie.

"Nice." She rolls her eyes at Brian.

Lisa watches as Angie takes the Irish crème from the cabinet and pours some into her coffee.

"Thanks." She adds some into her own coffee and then watches, almost horrified, as Brooke pours some into her hot chocolate. "Really?"

"Sure. Why not?"

"Daddy, Angie said Lisa's boyfriend is a bag of chips," Aidyn announces as she climbs up on Dave's lap. Jamie doesn't even look away from the TV.

"She did, huh?" Dave glances at Angie and grins. "Ken, hon, what kind of stuff you guys talkin' about in front of the munchkin?"

"I'm not a munchkin," Aidyn says fiercely.

"Of course, you're not." Dave makes a quick save. "I was talking about Ariel."

Aidyn laughs and leans back against Dave. Makenna hands him Aidyn's hot chocolate and then joins the rest of the girls in the dining room.

"How about Spoons?" Angie suggests. Piper, who had been about to go downstairs, turns at the mention of one of her favorite games.

"Yes!" Brooke nods.

"Spoons, it is. Grab some, Pipe."

The Spoons game, as always, is loud and tends toward vicious. Lisa tends to dive over the table whenever someone has a book of four of a kind and reaches for a spoon. Angie bites Piper more than once, and Makenna's diamond puts a gouge in Brooke's hand. They laugh, and when the hot drinks are gone, they open a bottle of wine, and the game gets louder. Finally, they are singing Christmas carols as they play, and they hear the guys griping in the living room, because they can't hear the TV. But it doesn't stop them. If anything, they are laughing harder and singing louder.

In the back of Angie's mind are other games like this, played at her mom's house or her aunts' houses, before her mom passed away. It feels good to savor the good memory of her mom, but she keeps it tucked away and out of sight and lets herself enjoy the night with her friends.

"Hey!" Makenna says as the Spoons game begins to wind down. Angie checks her watch and is shocked to see that it's after midnight. "Let's do dinner next week. Dinner and a movie. Just the girls."

"What night?" Brooke asks. Angie watches her drain her wineglass and wonders absently how much she's had to drink tonight. Brooke is usually the one to step back and drink soda. Angie hopes Jamie has not had much to drink tonight.

"I dunno." Makenna shrugs.

"How about Tuesday?" Angie says, because Tuesdays are good for her.

"Can't." Lisa shakes her head.

"What? Why not?"

"Jack and I have plans."

"You and Jack have plans for a Tuesday night?" Angie asks. "Really? Like you made a date for a Tuesday night?"

"We're ringing bells. For the Salvation Army."

"Seriously?" Brooke asks with a grin. "Where at?"

"The grocery store."

"You're gonna freeze your butts off," Makenna announces.

"Mm-hmm," Lisa nods, "but I'm pretty sure he'll warm me up later."

"Oh, oh!" Angie slaps the table. "Mr. Heatmiser's gonna warm her up, ladies."

Everyone around the table is laughing, even Piper, though a light blush floods her cheeks.

"Hey," Brooke turns to Lisa and her voice drops, "I talked to him."

Angie watches Lisa's happiness shift into something like dread.

"Great."

"It's okay." Brooke nods. "It's all okay."

"Woman," Dave says to Makenna as he walks into the dining room, a sleeping Aidyn on his shoulder. "Let's go."

"Does he always talk to you that way?" Angie asks Makenna. "Because that was kinda sexy."

Makenna snorts and rolls her eyes.

"You know," Angie goes on, "like in the movie *Top Gun*, where Goose says—"

"Well, okay, we know what's on Angie's mind, so I'm afraid you're all gonna have to go now," Brian interrupts Angie. He stands behind her and squeezes her shoulders.

"No, Brian, I'm leaving Dave here. Angie can have him tonight. You can have the night off."

"I didn't ask for the night off." Brian shakes his head. Makenna laughs and reaches out to take Brian's hand.

"Okay, you come home with me. We'll leave Angie and Dave here."

"Ohmygod," Piper groans and laughs. She ducks out of the room, her face beet red.

"It's always kinda fun to freak her out," Brian says with a shrug.

Angie stands up. "Fun and too easy."

"You guys are so mean to that kid." Lisa stretches and stands up.

"So, you guys are really ringing bells?" Angie asks Lisa, and this time the guys all laugh, even Jamie, just a little.

"Oh, come on."

Makenna giggles and looks at Dave. "Salvation Army bell. Tuesday."

Dave nods and looks at Lisa and mouths, "Sure."

"Not to say Jack's not gonna ring Lisa's bell a little later that night," Angie says as they all move toward the kitchen.

"Angie Edwards!" Lisa covers her face with her hands and groans. "Stop it."

"Yeah, Brian," Dave says with a wink. "We're gonna get outta your hair. I think Angie's got something on her mind."

"I heard that!" Piper yells from down the hall.

"Thanks," Angie tells Makenna when she hugs her goodbye. "It's been a fun night."

"It has," Makenna agrees, and then Angie stands in the front door, and cold air hovers around her. She watches her friends pile into their cars and leave. Lisa is by herself, and Angie wonders where Lisa said Jack was, if Lisa *had* said where he was. Or if Lisa would ever feel free to bring him around the group.

Around Jamie.

20

L isa

SHE STILL HASN'T TOLD HER FRIENDS THAT JACK IS divorced. Not that the divorce is the issue. She still hasn't told her friends that Jack has dated his ex-wife since the divorce. For two different time periods. Dated means slept with, of course. Lisa had known that from the word go, not because he'd come right out and told her. She's been in her fair share of relationships, so she knows what to expect, and she knows when men are lying, and she knows when men are still interested in their ex-wives.

In the beginning of their relationship, Jack was still interested in his ex-wife. Now she's not so sure. Maybe because she's falling for him, and she doesn't want to see any red flags. But maybe because there aren't any, and he's totally in love with Lisa.

She wonders, as she backs out of her drive, if Jack senses that she's holding part of herself back. If Jack sees any red flags when he looks at her. They've never said *I love you*, and Lisa's okay with that. But if they keep moving at this pace, will they be standing in the same place two months from now? Will things ever progress?

She hates being in this position. She hates that she will turn forty next year, and she's not married, and she wants to be married and so every man, every relationship, must be scrutinized like it is research rather than fun or even intense. Wondering about her relationship with Jack is so clinical, and Lisa just wants love. Love and happiness like her friends have.

Maybe since her parents divorced when she was so young, she should have more of a jaded outlook on marriage. Then again, maybe she does carry some fallout. Maybe that's part of the reason she hasn't ever allowed herself to really fall in love.

Except she has been in love. Just not with the right person.

She glances at her watch as she drives down Birch Street and makes a left turn at Twenty-Sixth. Breakfast? She's never been invited to Brooke and Jamie's for breakfast, and she thinks it's kind of weird. Jamie had caught her at school yesterday before she left. She'd been putting her grade book and a few files in her bag when she'd had that feeling that someone was watching her.

She'd found Jamie staring at her from the doorway of her classroom. They'd mumbled hellos to each other through the week, but things were certainly far from right. Lisa felt awkward now with him, not just because of the dressing down he'd given her over her behavior with

Jack, but also because she knows Brooke talked to him. She knows Brooke told him about how badly she wants her own family.

In retrospect, Lisa wonders if she'd have been better off keeping that completely to herself. Angie and Makenna don't know how important this is to her, and now suddenly Brooke knows. (Okay, not suddenly. Lisa told her, but *still*.) It's not that she fears Jamie will say anything to anyone. It just makes her feel like a crappy friend for not confiding in Angie and Makenna.

Jamie hadn't said much yesterday, in the door of her classroom. He was down, and he was sincere when he asked her to come over in the morning for breakfast. She could hear that much in his tone of voice. His eyes were a little sad, too, but he hadn't made eye contact with her any more than he absolutely had to.

She feels like she's being set up, but she shouldn't. She knows that Brooke talked to Jamie, so yes, that's what this breakfast is about. Jamie wants to talk to her about everything she's thinking about right now. About her wanting to get married and have children. She can't wait to hear what he has to say about her having children. She's sure it won't be anything good.

It feels weird to walk in empty-handed, too. True, she's not much of a cook. But she could've picked up some rolls or bagels or something. But Jamie had told her not to bring anything, just please come and have breakfast with him and Brooke.

If it were dinner time, or even lunchtime, she would take a bottle of wine or something. No, she wouldn't. That's what's freaking her out. She's looking at Jamie and Brooke Maczum like they are polite acquaintances, instead of the very, very good, close friends they really are. She hates feeling this way, thinking this way.

As if someone is watching for her, the garage door goes up as she pulls into their driveway. She turns her car off, takes a deep breath, and orders herself to quit being so ridiculous. Jamie is waiting at the back door for her.

"Hey." He closes the garage door behind her and then steps back to let her inside. "Lemme take your coat and purse."

She slips out of her coat and hands it to him.

"Look, before you even come further inside, I'm sorry."

"For what?" Lisa asks. She feels the blood drain from her face down to her feet, and she thinks she can't move. Why is he saying he's sorry? Because he's about to rip her ideas of motherhood to bits and pieces?

"For what I said the other day," he answers in a small voice. "For how I've been acting about Jack."

"It's okay." She swallows hard and avoids his eyes.

"It's not okay. I've been a dick about you and Jack from the beginning, and I'm sorry."

She laughs softly and finally looks up to meet his eyes. "You have been a dick about it."

He grins and reaches for her, and then she is caught up in his arms, pressed against him, her forehead pressed to his neck.

He is warm and solid and familiar, and it is a comfort to be in his arms, because it has been so long since he's acted like this. It's only when she's single that he will show her any affection; she's noticed that long ago.

It's a relief to her to be in his arms and not long for more. To not want to press her open mouth to his neck and run her hands over his shoulders and then back up over his chest.

Because *sometimes* she desperately wants to touch him that way. *Sometimes* she desperately wants more.

Maybe she doesn't feel that for him now because of Jack. Jack, who is with his daughter today. His daughter who lives with his ex-wife.

"C'min," he says softly, but he doesn't release her. Instead, he squeezes her again and kisses the top of her head, and finally, he lets her go, and she follows him through the kitchen.

He hands her a glass of juice, pushes a mug of coffee toward her, and nods to the kitchen table, telling her to sit down.

"Where's Brooke?"

"Upstairs," he answers. "I think she's looking for laundry in the boys' rooms."

Lisa nods, unable to deny that she's relieved Brooke is home.

"Smells good." She glances at the oven and sees the timer counting down.

"Blueberry muffins." He grins. "And bacon and eggs. Sound good?"

"Sounds like too much," she answers, but she's smiling. The house is warm, and the tree lights are on in the living room. Christmas music plays quietly.

"I've missed you."

She half-shrugs and nods and then shakes her head, wanting this portion of the morning to hurry by. She just wants to get back to who they used to be.

"Look," Jamie says, and he sits down at the table with

her. "I'm sorry that I've made you feel like you can't talk to me about this."

Instead of putting her at ease, his words make her feel even more self-conscious. Maybe this is where friendship between men and women gets complicated, and maybe she should cut the ties and walk away. Except she can't imagine her life without Jamie in it. She'd figured out long ago that he'd never be *the* man in her life. But he's definitely *part* of her life, and besides that, her life is good right now. Things with Jack are good, and maybe that's enough. Maybe she should quit worrying about Jamie running Jack off. If she digs her heels in, she can hang on. Maybe she should stop wondering about Jack and his ex-wife and wondering just where she and Jack are headed. Maybe if she stopped scrutinizing her feelings for him and just left herself *feel for him* things would progress naturally.

She still doesn't know what to say to Jamie. She hates that. This is *Jamie*. This is her best friend. The boy she'd talked to after her parents had divorced. The boy she'd confided in when she missed her mother, but didn't want to admit it, because she really wanted to hate her mother. The friend she'd told when she'd lost her virginity, when she'd been afraid she was pregnant when she was seventeen, when she'd been hurt and angry because her dad had moved away and remarried and had another child when Lisa was already twenty.

"Say something, Lisa. You're leaving me hanging out to dry." He stares into his coffee cup. She can read him like a well-loved book. He's scared that things have slipped too far out of hand, and she won't talk to him anymore as a friend.

"I don't know what to say," she answers finally. Her voice is scratchy, and she clears her throat and then looks up to meet his gaze. "You're like Super-Dad, and I feel like nothing I do would be good enough for you."

"First of all, nothing you do is for me to judge."

"But you would, Jamie," she whispers. "We all judge each other, even if we say we don't. It's human nature."

He shrugs and dips his head to acknowledge the truth in what she said. "Do you judge me? Is there something I do, other than how I've made you feel, that bothers you?"

When Lisa opens her mouth to argue, he shakes his head quickly. "No, I'm not even asking you to tell me what it is. I'm just saying maybe we do all judge each other, but that doesn't mean we don't believe in each other. It doesn't change a solid friendship."

She gives him a tiny nod, because he's right. Just because he might parent one way doesn't mean he wouldn't still care about her and support her if she did things a different way.

"I'm not Super-Dad," he continues. "Sometimes I feel like I'm an awful dad, and I think that's probably pretty common, too. So don't ever compare yourself to me and find anything lacking. That's unfair to all of us."

"But Jamie," Lisa takes a deep breath and looks at him again, "you had both parents around to show you how to do things. I didn't really even have a mom, and my dad wasn't very interested in what I was doing."

"So, you had parents to show you how not to do things." He takes a drink of his coffee. "And besides that, I know how that makes you feel, and I get it. But you're a very successful person, so I don't think your parents warped you too badly."

She laughs and rolls her eyes.

"Here's the thing," he says, and he leans back in his chair. "It's kind of a vicious circle. I always feel in the way when you're dating someone. I feel like an extra. And I don't like that. I want to be involved in what you're doing. And yeah, okay, I'm a little heavy-handed because I want to make sure you find someone to treat you right."

The oven timer begins beeping, and Jamie goes to take the muffins out. Lisa doesn't turn to watch him, but she waits for him to continue. It's nice to finally know what he's thinking every time he runs off one of her boyfriends. And yet, hadn't some tiny little part of her wanted it to be because he's so in love with her, he can't stand the thought of sharing her with anyone?

"So, I end up being a dick and pushing you away and then you don't talk to me. And so, we're back at the beginning."

Lisa looks up when Brooke walks into the kitchen.

"Hey!" Brooke grins. "I'm glad you could come."

"Find any more laundry?" Jamie asks her. He stands at the counter now, and there is bacon on the griddle in front of him.

"Stray socks," Brooke answers, and then she shivers and glances at Lisa. "Their rooms are so scary."

Lisa smiles, but she presses her lips together because what she wants to say is that Jamie's room was always beyond scary, and yet that implies an intimacy that just isn't there between them. Why put that out there and make Brooke wonder for no reason? Maybe if she didn't care so much about Brooke, she would.

"Laundry on a Saturday?" she asks instead, because she

thinks if she were home during the week, she'd want her weekends free of mundane household things like laundry.

Brooke's grin ratchets up another ten degrees. "I got a job. I start Monday, so I thought I'd get a head start on the laundry."

"You did?" Lisa knows Brooke has been thinking about going back to work. She knows Brooke's applied and interviewed at a few places, even the school. She hadn't been thrilled about that, but, she'd sensed Brooke's mixed feelings about being in the same work environment with her and Jamie, and she'd felt guilty about it, so she'd just smiled and paid lip service to how good it would be to all work together.

"Just a couple of days a week," Brooke answers. She takes the cup of coffee Jamie hands her, and Lisa can't help but notice how smooth the two of them are together. They have the kind of fluidity that only a couple who's been together for years could have, the kind she and Jamie have *sometimes*, even though they have nothing else that married couples have.

Actually, they're smooth together like she and Jack have become. She feels a rush of warmth as she realizes that she and Jack have moved into routine, and maybe that should be a bad thing because routine might mean boring. But for Lisa, right now, it means safety. Relationship. Love. Could that mean they're falling in love?

"At the health department."

"Brooke, that's great!" Lisa says and she means it, and not just because that means she won't be working with her and Jamie. But because the idea that she and Jack are settling into couplehood makes her feel light and happy inside. She stands and hugs Brooke and decides that maybe things are going to be fine.

Brooke will be happy working, she and Jamie can maintain their friendship at work just as it's always been, and she and Jack are a couple. And they might have a future.

"So, Lisa?" Jamie says. Lisa turns to watch him as he turns each strip of bacon with painstaking care.

"Hmm?" She refills her cup and leans on the counter.

"Are you in love with Jack?"

She is. She can honestly say she's in love with Jack. But saying yes will lead to a tougher question to answer. Is Jack in love with her? She doesn't know. She thinks he might be, but that's not enough to hang a diamond ring and baby bottle on.

"Yeah, Jamie," she answers truthfully. She meets his eyes, and she still loves Jack, but she feels a twinge of sadness because she knows she has to give up any thought of loving Jamie. "I am."

"Really?" Brooke asks her. "Really, really one hundred percent in love with him?"

Why is Brooke doing this to her? That sounds more like an Angie/Makenna direct hit.

"Is Jack the complete package? Marriage and a baby?"

Lisa sighs and feels that lightness inside her fall to her feet. She should have stayed home. She could be sleeping right now or doing her own laundry. Anything would be preferable to this.

"Because you don't have to rush into anything," Brooke tells her. "If you want a baby and you aren't sure about Jack, you don't have to rush into that."

Lisa stares at Brooke in silence. Because what can she

say? If she insists she's in love with Jack, she's going to start sounding like Lady MacBeth, protesting too much. Claiming too hard to be in love with Jack. And yes, of course, that other question is going to come up.

"You can do one without the other," Jamie says quietly.

"Brooke," Lisa groans and pushes her full coffee cup away. "We've talked about this. You know how I feel about it."

"About being a single mother?" Brooke asks. "Or about conceiving a child naturally?"

Lisa's mouth works to say something, but she can't find her voice.

"Because Jamie and I talked about this last night," Brooke continues when Lisa remains silent.

"And if you're serious about Jack, we're happy and we want that for you." Jamie lays the strips of bacon on a plate.

"But if you're not sure," Brooke says, "we want to make you an offer."

Lisa's head is buzzing like she's been drinking coffee spiked with something a hell of a lot stronger than creamer. She looks back at the table, glad to see Jamie hadn't gotten out of the kitchen with her coat and purse.

Time to go. She doesn't even want to hear the offer. Nothing good is going to happen in the next two minutes, unless Lisa can get her keys and get the hell out of dodge.

"Let me father your baby," Jamie says as she turns back to the table.

"Are you out of your mind?" Lisa turns back to look at Jamie. She's shaking so hard, she wonders absently if she should drive.

"Women do this all the time, Lisa," he says calmly.

"You've heard of women being surrogate mothers. This is—"

Lisa shakes her head. "No. This is…no." She picks up her purse and coat and stalks to the back door.

"Lisa, wait."

"No." Lisa swallows hard and shakes her head again.

She leaves them staring after her and swallows hard and shakes her head again. Still carrying her coat, she moves on autopilot. Opens the garage door and digs in her purse for her keys as she walks to her car.

Set-up, all right. Complete friggin' ambush.

Her hands shake on the wheel, but she zips out of the driveway and heads for home.

21

M akenna

TODAY STARTS OUT WITH A HEADACHE THAT HITS HER DEEP in the back of her neck, and Makenna wonders how she can have a tension headache before she even gets out of bed. Dave was awake at eight, and he'd curled up close behind her. Spooning. That thought had made her think of the girls' game of Spoons the other night, which had at least brought a smile to her face. But, it hadn't lasted.

It's after nine, and Makenna has so much to do, she gets up. She rolls her shoulders, wishing that would magically make the headache go away. It doesn't, of course, and maybe nothing will but time. She turns the shower water on, and as she is undressing, Dave opens the door and wiggles his eyebrows at her. Again, she has to laugh, and Dave takes this as an invitation.

Steam clouds the bathroom, and Makenna pushes everything from her mind but the moment. The hot water, Dave's hands and mouth. His body hard under her wandering hands. The bathroom door is locked, and the girls are sleeping still, and the presents and the last minute shopping will all wait. When the orgasm drains her, she feels the tension melt from her neck and shoulders. It has been a long time since they've played in the shower, and Makenna wishes they could have more moments like this.

They could have more moments like this, she thinks, but they never slow down enough to make them. There is always something else that needs to be done. Somewhere they need to go. She is exhausted when she goes to bed at night and sometimes, even more exhausted when she gets up in the morning.

They finish their shower in lukewarm water, and Dave says how Ariel will have a fit when she realizes she will have a cold shower. Laughing and acting like kids, like the teenagers they used to be, they dress and go through the morning ritual side by side. Dave shaves and flosses and brushes his teeth as Makenna blows her hair dry and puts on makeup that she never leaves the house without.

She makes coffee as he gulps down a glass of juice and eats a quick bowl of cereal.

"Where are you going?" she asks him when he's putting his shoes on.

"Taking the truck in for an oil change," he tells her. "Going to the bank. Maybe a little shopping."

The last makes her smile.

"I'll check back before I do that. See if the girls are up."

He leans over and kisses her cheek. "Maybe they'll wanna do a little shopping with me."

"Need a list?" Makenna asks with a grin.

"With Ariel along? Nope."

Makenna laughs, because she knows that anything she ever mentions she wouldn't mind having, Ariel tells Dave to get for her. Even if it's something ridiculous like a new gadget for the garden. A garden they don't even have.

"I'll call in a bit." Dave kisses her again, this time on her lips, and the kiss drags into something deeper and warmer.

"Yuck!"

They laugh and pull away. Ariel is standing in the kitchen with her nose turned up.

"I'll be back in a while to get you and your sister," Dave tells her. "Christmas shopping for Mom."

Ariel's face lights up, and Makenna knows Dave will make a day of it. They'll do lunch, and they'll shop, and Makenna feels a twinge of loneliness. Silly, because they are shopping for her, but she'd like to go with them, just to be out of the house and involved in the holiday bustle.

Which is stupid, because she doesn't want to be with crowds of people, and she doesn't want to spend any more money, and she's had it with all of the above, and she still has stuff to wrap.

And yet, somehow it sounds better than being here alone.

"Love you," Dave says. She tells him she loves him, and then he's gone. Ariel grins at her and then hurries down the hall to get her shower.

Makenna pours herself a bowl of Rice Krispies just as Ariel shrieks from the bathroom. Makenna texts Dave and tells him Ariel's not happy with the cold shower, and Dave responds with a smiley face. Aidyn comes out of her bedroom rubbing her eyes and asks Makenna where Daddy is.

Makenna hugs her and pulls out a barstool. Aidyn climbs up to sit down as Makenna pours her a small bowl of cereal.

"Daddy's running errands, and then he's coming back to get you guys. You wanna go shopping with Dad and Ariel?"

"What about you, Mom?" Aidyn asks as Makenna adds milk to her bowl.

"I have plenty to do here." Makenna ignores that little prick of sadness. "In fact, maybe you guys should fly to France to shop for me."

Aidyn grins. "You want jewels?"

"You bet I do."

"And fur coats?"

"Three, please," Makenna answers.

"I'm full," Aidyn says and pushes her bowl away.

"One bite doesn't make you full," Makenna answers. "You have to eat half of that, or you can't go with Daddy."

Aidyn rolls her eyes, and Makenna thinks of Piper and laughs to herself. It must be something girls are born with, the talent to speak a thousand words with a roll of their eyes.

Later, the girls and Dave are gone, and Makenna is at the dining room table, wrapping presents. She's almost finished wrapping the Santa stuff, but she figures today is a good day to take care of the rest of it.

Probably Ariel doesn't believe anymore. Probably *Aidyn* doesn't believe. Seems kids are ripping on the whole idea of Santa before they hit kindergarten these days. It makes her sad to think that her girls, at least Ariel, are too old to believe in Santa.

Maybe it's the music, but Makenna feels the sting of tears as she wraps. Jim Brickman's piano music is usually so soothing, but today it's pulling her down. She finishes wrapping a doll for Aidyn and sets it in Aidyn's pile and then goes to change the song.

The doorbell rings before she can do it. She swallows hard and takes a deep breath before she opens the door. She doesn't feel much like explaining her mood to anyone, so she has to appear *normal* when she opens the door.

"Hey!" Angie grins and steps inside and pushes the door closed before the wind can blow any snow inside. It's beautiful outside, but Makenna hardly notices. "Where's everybody at?"

"Christmas shopping," Makenna answers. Angie takes her coat and boots off. "I think I was the smart one. It's cold out there."

"It's two today," Angie agrees. "You're lucky. Brian shops for me the day before Christmas Eve."

Makenna takes Angie's coat and lays it over the couch. She squats down in front of the stereo to change the CDs. Angie grabs the home phone and punches in a number. Makenna assumes she is ordering pizza.

"Sausage okay with you?" Angie asks, and Makenna nods and loads the CD player with upbeat CDs like Chris Isaak and The Rat Pack and Mariah Carey.

"This is pretty paper," Angie decides when she hangs up the phone after ordering a pizza for delivery. She sits down across the table from Makenna and watches her wrap.

Makenna sighs and nods. She loves Angie to death, but sometimes it's so damned hard to put her game face on.

"Look at this." She shows Angie a roll of wrapping paper she'd just bought two days ago. It's navy with silver packages on it, and even though Christmas is almost here, she'd bought it and two other rolls because she liked it. She'd use it next year, if nothing else.

"Ooh, I love it," Angie gushes. "Where'd you get it?"

"No idea," Makenna answers truthfully. "What are you on?"

"Vacation."

"Seriously?"

"Oh yeah." Angie nods. "Off all week."

"Lucky you."

Angie helps her wrap, and for a while, there is only the Christmas music between them. Makenna feels the moment when she settles down. When the sadness goes and the tension, which has built again, eases.

"I hate Christmas," she mumbles as she tapes the corner of a box for Ariel. Inside the box is a set of golf clubs. Dave had decided Ariel should try golf, since she's already got a new bat and batting helmet and glove.

"No, you don't," Angie answers, and without looking, Makenna imagines she is rolling her eyes. "You're like Queen Christmas."

"I like pre-Christmas," Makenna tells her. "Well, I used to."

Angie waits for her to keep talking. Makenna rubs the back of her neck. "I still have Dave's stuff to wrap. Mom and Dad's stuff. I need to get a check to Dave's brother for the new recliner we got his parents. Dave asked me to bake for the guys at work for Monday. I have—"

"Breathe," Angie says softly.

Makenna laughs and sits back in her chair. Her stomach growls, and she's glad that Angie showed up and ordered pizza.

"I hate the day. Christmas Day." She lays her head on the back of the chair. "Because it's the end."

"I know."

"It goes faster and faster each year, and I feel like I don't get it anymore. I don't feel that magic anymore. The way holidays make you feel when you're a kid. I hate losing that, Ang."

"Ken, you spend so much time worrying. You keep looking for the magic, and one of these days, it's gonna bite you on the ass."

Makenna smiles sadly.

"So, we don't have the magic of childhood. We don't look out the window waiting to see Santa. We don't imagine flying reindeer and the North Pole. We have our own magic."

Makenna stares at Angie, unconvinced.

"We're wrapping presents together. Listening to Christmas music. We decorated Lisa's tree together. The drive through the North Pole the other night."

"That was a blast," Makenna agrees.

"That's our magic," Angie tells her. "All the littlest moments. Adults find Christmas magic in all of the small hours."

Makenna blinks hard and nods. "I know you're right," she says softly, because she does know Angie's right. She could rattle off hundreds more magic moments in her heart. "But I hate how a square of paper dictates our lives. December's almost over. I hate January."

"The calendar doesn't rule our lives," Angie answers. "It's what we write on it that makes the difference."

Makenna raises her eyebrows and reaches to pick up the present on the table.

"Is that anything like a snake bite? Gettin' bit on the ass by magic?"

"I don't know," Angie says, "but if it is, I'm not suckin' any venom out. You'll have to ask Dave to help you out."

ngie

BRIAN AND THE KIDS ARE CHRISTMAS SHOPPING, SO ANGIE calls Makenna and Lisa and invites them over. It's an impromptu girls' night, and sometimes impromptu things are more fun and more relaxed than something that's been planned months ahead of time. Planning implies that something is important, and that adds expectation, which for Angie, can often lead to disappointment.

Angie had mentioned calling Brooke, but Lisa had asked her not to. Lisa doesn't seem inclined to tell them why she didn't want Brooke around. In fact, Lisa isn't talking much at all. She looks worn out, and her mouth is set in a hard, straight line. Angie's not sure she's seen her smile once since she got here.

Angie glances at Makenna now, wondering if she's

noticed that Lisa seems preoccupied. She kind of hopes that Makenna doesn't say anything, because Lisa acts like she'll explode if anyone pokes at her. Sometimes it's okay to pry something out of someone, but sometimes things are better left alone.

Makenna seems content to stare at the TV. Angie wonders how she's doing. She's reached that point in the holidays where she's a little sad and a little restless. Angie's witnessed it every year since they were kids. But she'd never heard Makenna say she hates Christmas until just the other day.

Angie supposes it's true that misery loves company, because she was glad to know she's not alone when she feels that way. She doesn't *always* hate Christmas, and she knows Makenna doesn't either, and yet she can sure relate to that feeling at times.

They're watching *It's a Wonderful Life*, and Angie remembers back when Piper was about eight, they watched it together. Curled up on the couch, sharing a big bowl of popcorn. Last year, they'd watched *The Holiday* together and shared popcorn, just two nights before Christmas. If Makenna were to question Christmas magic again, Angie would probably present these two nights that have burned themselves into her brain as evidence to prove her point. Or maybe the nights she and Zach watched Christmas cartoons when he was a little boy.

The tree lights are the only lights on in the house, and they are watching the movie on the flat screen TV in the basement. The fireplace is turned on—Angie thinks the gas fireplace is the best feature of her house—and they are full from Mort's fried chicken.

It's a cozy night, and it reminds Angie of the days

when it was just the three of them, before they'd gotten to know Brooke.

"Guys."

Lisa sits up straight and rubs her face with her hands.

"What's the matter? You can't go home yet," Makenna says, and it sounds like she's joking. But she's looking at Angie, and it's obvious she's worried about Lisa, too. "It's too early."

Lisa sighs and then folds her hands in her lap.

"Look. This isn't easy for me to say, but," she stands up and wanders closer to the fireplace. "I'm skipping Christmas this year."

Angie and Makenna glance at each other again. Angie is tempted to make a joke and refer to the John Grisham novel about skipping Christmas and how well that worked out for the family involved. But she senses something huge is about to happen, so she says nothing.

"I need some time to myself."

"Isn't this something you would normally say to Jack?" Angie asks.

Lisa shakes her head. "I'm serious. I have so much going on, you can't even begin to know. I need to be alone to sort it all out."

"What do you mean?"

"I really don't wanna talk about it." Lisa clears her throat. "I don't. I just wanted to give you a head's up. I'm not gonna be around for Christmas."

"Are you going somewhere with Jack?" Angie asks her.

"Do you ever listen?" Lisa snaps. "Alone. I need some time to myself."

Angie stands up, surprised by what Lisa said and a little angry. She's *always* listened. To all of them. Lisa and

Makenna are the ones who tend to jump in without listening first.

"Okay." Angie shrugs. "If that's what you want."

Lisa stares at her for a minute, as if she expects Angie to change her mind. She glances at Makenna and then turns her back to them to go upstairs.

"You know where we are, Lisa," Angie says quietly, "if you decide you need us."

Lisa stops with one foot on the bottom step.

Angie looks away from Lisa. Makenna is still sitting on the couch. She's staring at the Christmas tree. This tree is Angie's favorite, the one with the ornaments the kids have made through the years and the Hallmark ornaments. Every ornament on this tree has a story, and Angie could sit down and tell each one in perfect detail.

"He offered to be a surrogate father," Lisa says quietly. She stands with her back to Angie and Makenna, but Angie sees from the heave in her shoulders that she's trying to control her emotions.

"Jack?" Angie asks, but she knows she's wrong. Only one person could make that offer and hurt Lisa so deeply.

Lisa shakes her head and turns around to look at them. Her eyes are bright with tears twenty years in the making.

"Jamie." She mouths his name, and Angie waits for her to shatter and fall to the floor and lay waiting for Angie to sweep her away.

Tread softly, Angie reminds herself. At the moment, Lisa is a grenade, and Angie holds her in her hand. One wrong word, and the pin is pulled, and all hell breaks loose. If certain words are said, the destruction might just be too much to fix.

Lisa had just accused her of not listening, so she decides to say nothing, to wait for Lisa to share more.

"Twenty-five years." Lisa sniffles and the tears start to fall. "Twenty-five years of loving him, and he throws it in my face that he would father my child."

"Lisa," Angie whispers, and she's so scared to say another word. Makenna watches and waits, wanting Angie to take charge. "Maybe it's time you and Jamie really talked. Maybe you have to tell him how you feel about him, damn the consequences."

"But that's just it, Angie!" Lisa wipes at her eyes. "I finally feel like I belong with someone. It hit me Saturday. The fact that I could live with Jack. That I love waking up with him. That I love sleeping next to him. Sharing dinner with him. Talking to him. We laugh together. It finally clicked for me, and then Jamie…"

Lisa swallows hard and looks away. "And then Jamie has the nerve to question my commitment to Jack. My feelings for Jack. And he says I shouldn't be rushing into anything, and that maybe I've latched onto Jack just because I want a baby, and if that's the case, he'll father my child for me."

Angie is lost. She feels like she's turned on a movie during the last hour, when things are unraveling so fast there's no way to catch up.

She starts to say something. She starts to say that she didn't realize how badly Lisa wanted a baby, but she catches herself. Because this moment isn't about the hurt she feels for being left out. This is about Lisa and Jamie and maybe how the group of seven is about to implode.

Maybe, Angie thinks, that's best. Maybe if we all go our separate ways, it will empower Lisa to find what she wants. Maybe sometimes this is too much work. Makenna is the peacekeeper and maybe that's stressful. But Angie is hands-on with counsel and advice and leadership, and she doesn't know how it came to be that they all look to her to take charge of situations out of the ordinary.

But maybe washing her hands of it and burrowing deep into her family life with Brian and the kids is the answer.

"Maybe he didn't mean it as an insult." Makenna speaks for the first time, and typical Makenna, she wants to defend Jamie to Lisa. As far as Angie is concerned, there's no defending something like this. Married men don't father single women's children. For any reason. Other than an itch that might have something to do with mid-life.

"Kenna, don't," Lisa pleads. "Please don't. Jamie's being his usual self, and he's being an ass, and I am begging you not to defend him."

"Offering to father your child makes him an ass?" Makenna frowns.

"He only offered after I said I was in love with Jack."

Angie sighs. "That's a pretty heavy-handed way to get rid of Jack, don't you think?"

"You don't know the half of it."

And that's the problem. Apparently Lisa has been knee-deep in some heavy thinking, and Angie and Makenna know nothing about it.

"No, we don't," Angie says quietly. "But we'd like to."

Lisa groans.

"In for a penny, in for a pound," Angie reminds her.

"Is it possible to love two people? Two men? At the same time?"

Angie moves quickly when Lisa's knees buckle. She backs Lisa to the steps and sits her down. Angie sits on the floor and stares at Lisa.

"Do you love Jack?"

Lisa nods. She wipes at her face again, smearing mascara and eyeliner.

"And are you in love with Jamie?"

"Yes." The word is a sob, and it breaks Angie's heart. She'd like to slap some sense into Jamie if he made this offer to break up Lisa's relationship with Jack.

"Then it's possible," Angie answers quietly. "The question is what're you gonna do about it?"

"Do about it?" Lisa repeats. "What the hell does that mean? I'm not gonna do anything about it."

Again Angie senses that it is better to wait Lisa out, though it's a struggle to stay calm. It's not fair of Lisa to play this hand and to need to talk and not share whatever the beginning is.

"He's married, Ang," Lisa sobs. "I would never do anything to hurt his family."

"What gave him the right to make that offer, Lisa?" Angie asks. "I don't understand what's going on."

Lisa blinks and looks away. Angie thinks that even when Lisa cries, she's pretty. She still wonders why Jamie and Lisa aren't together. As much as she likes Brooke, and she does, she doesn't understand how Lisa and Jamie could have loved each other all of these years and still missed the chance to spend their lives together.

"I love your kids," Lisa whispers. "I love all your kids, Ang, but it's not enough."

"Of course, it's not enough," Angie answers.

Lisa seems taken aback by Angie's words. She closes

her eyes. Maybe to calm herself, maybe to shut Angie out. At this point, Angie can't read her, and she's beginning to feel like there might be a lot about Lisa that she doesn't know.

"I feel like everyone looks at me and sees a professional. A cold, hard-hearted career woman. And that being alone now, with no husband and no children, is what I deserve. For the choices I made in my life."

Angie raises her eyebrows, unable to hide that she is hurt by Lisa's words. "Everyone. So you think that Makenna and I judge you. You think that we think you deserve to be alone, because you went to college and got a degree and put it to use? Or maybe we should throw your mom into the mix, right? Let me guess, Makenna and I think you'd be a horrible mom because your mom left you when you were young, so how could you possibly know how it's done?"

Lisa sinks her perfect teeth into her lower lip and stares at Angie sadly. "Okay, I made a mistake. But I was afraid to talk about it, Angie."

"What I'd like to know is when I've ever been such a bitch to you to make you think I'd judge you."

"You're not me," Lisa says quietly. "You have the life. You have everything I wish I had. And until you are me, you can't know what it feels like to watch your friends live successful lives and feel...flawed...because you don't."

"Bullshit, Lisa." Angie shakes her head. "I'm not you. But here's what I've always thought about you. You're beautiful. Inside and out. You're loyal. Compassionate. And you work at a job you love, while you wait for the right guy to come along."

Angie stands up and slips her hands in the pockets of her jeans.

"I've always thought you were smart and patient, and that one day you'd have so much love to give a child."

"Ang—" Lisa says as Angie steps past her and climbs the stairs. She's had enough. For the first time in twenty years, certainly for the first time since they've all grown up and graduated from high school, Angie's had enough of her friends and the drama. She wants them to leave, because right now what she wants most is to be alone.

23

M akenna

MAKENNA CAN HEAR ANGIE UPSTAIRS. SHE'S straightening the kitchen, rinsing the dishes they'd used and already rinsed, and loading the dishwasher. This is new. Makenna hasn't seen Angie upset like this, not by something she or Lisa has said, in a good twenty years.

Angie's entitled to the anger, the hurt. Makenna feels that way, too. But maybe now isn't the time to acknowledge that. What she'd really like to do is go home. She has no desire to touch this mess of Lisa and Jamie and God only knows what else, and she knows Angie's upset, and it's not that she doesn't want to comfort her. It's more that she knows Angie doesn't want to be comforted. Not right now. Angie wants them to leave, so she can be alone.

Makenna would feel the same way if this were taking place at her house.

But, she can't get up and walk upstairs and leave Lisa sit. She doesn't want to be mean about it. She's just exhausted, and she wishes she were at home in bed.

"So." She sighs and flops back on the couch. Lisa is still sitting on the steps. "I'm assuming that you've been talking to Jamie about all of this?"

Lisa hesitates but finally says, "No."

"Brooke."

"Yeah."

Makenna's kind of glad Angie wasn't down here to hear that. She doesn't move from the couch, doesn't even look Lisa's way.

"Sort of like looking into a mirror," Lisa mumbles. "I see all the flaws. And you guys know me too well to not see them. Brooke doesn't."

"I don't see flaws, Lisa, and even if I did, I wouldn't catalogue them."

Makenna hears Lisa sigh or groan or something. Lisa is irritated now, too.

"C'mon Makenna," she says and Makenna can tell she's gotten to her feet, and she's walking toward Makenna and the couch. "Get off Angie's high horse. Are you telling me Angie and I know everything there is to know about you? And I don't mean everything you did in grade school and high school. I don't mean how you got drunk after the prom and got sick, and I don't mean how you spanked Ariel when she was three, and you felt bad about it. I mean something deep inside. Don't you keep something for just you?"

Makenna looks over the back of the couch and sees the desperation on Lisa's face. She sighs and feels her resolve cave.

"Of course, I do," she relents. She scoots sideways on the couch, silently inviting Lisa to sit down. "Everyone does, Lisa. But this...this is something big for you. And you know Angie and I don't look down on you because of your career. We've never assumed you just didn't want kids."

It's Lisa's turn to deflate. She climbs over the back of the couch, and Makenna has to giggle and glance at the steps. Angie would have a fit if she'd seen that. Lisa's mouth tilts to an almost smile, but it doesn't quite make it.

"I know." She nods. "I do. I've been telling myself this for weeks. I just. I didn't want this," Lisa waves her hands in circles, "to become the center of everything. It's just me. It's just something I want. I don't want everyone to focus on me wanting a child."

Makenna shrugs a shoulder, but she nods. "I get that. We don't have to make it a group thing. But I wish you'd have talked to me and Ang about it."

Lisa nods. "Brooke and I got to talking one night, and one thing led to another, and before I knew it, I'd said just about everything."

"Kinda weird."

"It is. But things with me and Jamie aren't quite as star-crossed as you make them out to be, Ken. I love him. I've always loved him. Some days I'm so far in love with him, I know I'll never get over it."

Makenna studies Lisa's face for a moment. She's definitely exhausted, because Makenna's never seen her look so undone. There are dark circles under her eyes that she's attempted to cover with makeup. The whites of her eyes are lined with red. Even her hair is messed, but Makenna figures that she's been sitting on the steps dragging her fingers through it and probably pulling it in frustration.

Knowing what it is to feel like you're under a microscope, Makenna looks away. Back at Angie's tree. She wonders what Angie is doing now, while she and Lisa sit downstairs without her.

"But I would never do anything to hurt him," Lisa continues. "And I know that he loves Brooke, and that getting involved with me in anyway would end up hurting him."

"I've never meant to give you the impression I believe that about you. That you would have an affair with him."

"I've done it before," Lisa reminds her.

"You were still a kid, and you didn't even realize he was married."

"Still. It was a stupid mistake."

"A mistake," Makenna agrees with a small nod. "I've never thought you would do that. It's just that sometimes, being outside of you two, I see it. The way you look at each other. Watch each other. And I hate that you can't both have what you want."

"I'm not desperate, Makenna. I'm not desperate to be with him. It's not like I'll never be happy without him."

Makenna lays her head back on the couch.

"I guess I just wish he could let me go. Completely. Because it's not fair that when I feel like I'm moving on again, he pulls me back. I don't know why he does it, but it's not fair. And maybe it means I need to break that tie."

Makenna's heart skips, but Lisa's right. The situation

has become emotionally untenable for her. Something has to give.

"How did you go from wanting your own child to Jamie offering to father a baby?" Makenna asks quietly. "If I can ask."

"I honestly have no idea. Brooke asked me if she could tell him what we'd been talking about." Lisa shrugs. "I said yes, and this is what they came up with."

"They?"

"Oh, yeah. Brooke was standing right there when he suggested this."

Makenna stares at Lisa, shocked to learn that Brooke was involved.

"So. Was he offering to..." Makenna raises her eyebrows, "donate sperm for artificial insemination? Or..."

"I have no idea. I told him he was out of his mind, and I picked up my stuff, and I walked out."

"Wow."

"No kidding."

"What about Jack?"

Lisa shrugs. She stands up and moves to examine an ornament on the tree. It's a bear, with a big round tummy and it says Mom, 2001. Makenna feels a jolt inside, like a spike to her heart. Lisa's endured fifteen years of this. Of not belonging to the motherhood club. Of conversations about pregnancy and labor and delivery. Of Christmas ornaments that say Mom. Of baseball games and Christmas programs and homemade Mother's Day cards.

Of course, Lisa loves their kids, but how it must hurt her to not have her own children.

"I don't know," Lisa mumbles. "I don't know how he feels about me. He's divorced. Did you know that?"

"Huh-uh."

"He's divorced. And he has a sixteen-year-old daughter that he doesn't see very often."

"Have you met her?"

"No." Lisa presses her lips together and kind of smiles, but it's not a happy smile. "When we first started seeing each other, he was kind of seeing his ex-wife."

"Oh."

"I don't think he is now."

"You haven't asked?"

Lisa shrugs. "Rockin' the boat, ya know?"

"You do have a lot on your plate."

"I do. And now I've pissed Angie off." Lisa laughs, but the sound breaks and so does Lisa, and she's crying again. "I didn't mean to hurt you guys, Makenna. It's just...it's a deep...fear, I guess. I knew you guys would understand, but there was just this part of me..."

"I know," Makenna says quietly, "and so does Angie."

"I haven't seen her that pissed in, like, forever."

"We put a lot on her."

"She's so strong."

"She is," Makenna agrees. "But so are we. She'll be fine."

"I don't know what to do, Makenna," Lisa whispers.

Makenna hears something, and she knows then that Angie has been sitting at the top of the steps listening to them. Angie just stood up, and maybe the sound Makenna heard was Angie's bones popping because even though this feels like junior high drama, they're all adults, and the years are catching up to them, and Makenna knows that Angie still won't come back down.

Because maybe sometimes they all need a little space.

ngie

THE OFFICE CHRISTMAS PARTY IS ANOTHER ONE OF THOSE things that Angie dreads like a wine hangover and ends up enjoying once it's happening. Not so much this year, though. Her butt propped on her friend Erin's desk, she quietly watches everyone else enjoying themselves. Some are drinking grape juice from lovely plastic ware, and some are drinking coffee that someone made a run for. Angie's holding a big espresso, and occasionally, she takes a sip from it. She's not worried about what the espresso might do to her. Actually, she's hoping maybe it'll be enough to get her through the next few days. Including Christmas.

She's thinking how if she drinks this whole damned big cup of coffee, she'll have to stop five times to pee on the fifteen minute drive home. Who buys this size, anyway? Coffee always goes right through her, and she thinks maybe she should have opted for a glass of "bubbly." Not much to feel bubbly about right now. Even if it is three days before Christmas.

This part of the bank is decked out, as always. Two of her colleagues sit on the desks, shoes kicked off, talking trash about football. Her friend Erin is trying to get a sing-along started. Angie wonders what it's like out front, where the customers are. The office party, back here in the maze of cubicles where no customers are allowed, gets a bit wild, and Angie used to be involved up to her neck.

Erin's already wormed Tom, the guy at the next cubicle. Angie had known Erin dumped the entire box of rubber bands over the wall the second she'd heard Tom explode with a *son-of-a-bitch, Erin!* She'd laughed to herself, but she hadn't even looked away from her computer screen.

They're exchanging Secret Santa gifts today, and Angie's Secret Santa is sick, so she sits and watches everyone open gifts. In the past six days, she's gotten a bag of Dove dark chocolates (she'd eaten half the bag the day she found it on her desk,) a mint Mocha (thank God, just a large, or she'd have passed the morning work hours in the bathroom,) a gift card for the movies, a bag of Dove chocolates with caramel, a small inspirational book about finding happiness in the odd moments of life, and a gift card that would probably cover lunch and coffee at the café next door. Not too damned bad. In fact, so good that Angie doesn't mind that her Secret Santa isn't here today. Other than wondering who it is, of course.

She thinks it must be Camryn Shaw, from bookkeeping, because she hasn't seen her all day. Marilyn East, from accounts payables, had liked the hand-blown glass Christmas ornament Angie had given her today. Angie had almost brought in a bottle of wine, one of her and Brian's favorites, but then she'd found out Marilyn and her husband don't drink. So, she'd stopped at the jewelry store on the way home last night and picked up the ornament. She'd had it gift wrapped, because she had no desire to wrap another thing this year.

The kids must be home by now. They'd gotten out early today. Angie kind of hates that she'd missed Zach's Christmas party at school, but then again, she doesn't. The very fact that she doesn't care much makes her feel bad. Guilty. Like a bad mom. Not that Zach would care, anyway. He hadn't wanted her around at school since he'd been in third grade.

It's hard for her to believe Christmas is just a few days away. The season flew by this year, and yes, she's heard how it goes so much faster the older you get. Her mom used to tell her that all the time. Her dad still does, along with her aunts and uncles. But this year it really did go fast.

In a couple of years, Piper will be away at college. True, she'll be home for Christmas. But still, Piper leaving will change everything. Angie's not ready for that moment. She's very proud of her, and she knows she's going to be successful no matter what career path she chooses. But she's still not ready to let Piper go down that life path.

When Piper goes to college, Zach'll start high school. She misses having little ones around. She misses the feeling of holding a baby close and rocking a baby to sleep. She doesn't say that around Piper. Piper hasn't really dated anyone; she goes out with groups of friends, but there's never been any one boy she's been interested in. Still, no need to wish for babies for about ten more years.

Thinking about babies makes Angie think about Lisa. She doesn't know when Lisa and Makenna left the other night. She'd sat at the top of the steps and listened to them talk. It was nice to hear Makenna defend her, but then Lisa didn't really attack her. Actually, after listening to them, Angie'd understood exactly where Lisa was coming from. But understanding didn't take away the hurt.

She'd gone into her bedroom and sat and stared out the window. At the snow-covered ground. At the snow in the bare tree limbs. The lights on the neighbors' houses. Wondered exactly where Brian and the kids were. Missed her mom. When she'd wandered out of her room later, the basement lights were off, and Lisa and Makenna were gone.

Makenna had called her the next morning, and Angie had told her she was fine and not to worry about it. It was unlike Makenna, but she let it go at that. She didn't harp on Angie to forgive Lisa or to call Lisa. Angie knows Makenna had known she was listening to their conversation, but she also thinks maybe Makenna had let it go because she felt the same way.

Lisa had dropped by the next afternoon. Brian and the kids were watching football. Angie was making home-made soup and doing a crossword puzzle, and Lisa had come in and opened her mouth to apologize. Maybe to explain. But Angie'd cut her off and told her not to worry about it, everything was fine. They'd even hugged, and *really*, it was all okay.

But then again, each little cut leaves a mark, and Angie still feels a little sting each time she thinks of it. She'll never use Lisa's distrust against her, but she'll never forget that Lisa had chosen to confide in Brooke, either. Angie's not one for revenge, and she doesn't hold grudges, because life is too short for hard feelings.

But she still feels just a little different inside.

"Hey."

Angie looks at Erin and stands up. She grins, because even though she thinks she'd be just plain empty inside if someone sliced her open, she's got a damned good game face. And she wears it well.

It doesn't escape her that her game face and Lisa's fear are very much alike. Unfair of her, but then if she's going to feel it and keep it to herself, who the hell cares? Makenna and Lisa will never know, so she's going to choose to be unfair.

"You wanna go out for a drink?" Erin asks. Angie glances at the clock on the wall, surprised that it is quitting time.

"No," she says with a laugh. "Are you nuts? It's two degrees out there, and I've been ready for sweatpants and the fireplace since about eleven o'clock this morning."

"You're such a wuss," Erin says good-naturedly.

"It's old age."

Erin laughs. "Well, if you're not going to have a drink with me, I have some last minute shopping to do. See ya later."

Last minute shopping. Angie can't imagine. She bundles up in her coat, grabs her purse, and heads for freedom. As she navigates the snow that no amount of shoveling and salt has removed, she thinks about how she and her mom used to do last minute shopping.

There was always something her mom remembered she'd wanted to get her dad. At the eleventh hour. She and her mom would always say it would be a quick trip, but then they'd shop for an hour or two, and they'd end up grabbing dinner together and then talking until it was damned near ten o'clock. Her dad and Brian would always wonder how she and her mom could always find so much to talk about.

Maybe that's what's wrong with me, Angie thinks now. Mom's been gone for two years, and I haven't talked to her in two years, and I have all of this stuff inside me that I need to say to her, and I can't. Because I know she can't answer me.

She sits in her car, waiting for it to get warm even though she knows it won't even be warm by the time she pulls into the garage.

That's not it, though. Angie's not full of words she might have shared with her mom. She's stopped thinking in terms of talking to her mom, and so now she's empty, and that's left her wide open for this huge, aching loneliness inside her.

What she wouldn't give just to talk to her mom. Right now. For ten minutes. Five minutes.

Not true, she thinks as she backs out of her parking space. Five minutes, ten minutes, ten years would never be enough if she knew she was just going to lose her mom all over again.

The hell of it is knowing that one day she will lose her dad. He's healthy now, and he's relatively happy, as happy as he can be without her mom. But death is part of life, and so one day, she'll lose him, too. And then she'll be alone.

Well, not alone. She has Brian and Piper and Zach, and they fill her completely with love and joy and pride.

But losing a parent is like being set adrift in a world that suddenly seems foreign and cold and frightening.

"I love you, Mom," she whispers, and she realizes she is crying.

Angie's mom did this. She'd survived her mother's death when Angie was nine. It had been hard for her; Angie remembers wanting to help her mom through the grief but not knowing how. But her mom had done it; she would, too.

She tucks her mom back inside her heart and drives home to her family.

25

L isa

HE'D SAID IT LAST NIGHT. LISA CAN STILL HEAR HIM, whispering to her. She hasn't let any man ever get close enough to say *I love you* after the fiasco when she was so young and stupid and got involved with a married man. But last night, she and Jack had lain together on the couch and watched *The Family Stone* and of course she'd cried, because even though some people think she's cold-hearted (she's heard her students say it) she's a sap and a sucker for a tear-jerker movie.

They'd made love when the movie was over. Right there on the couch, with the DVD trailer thing repeating over and over and the tree lights on, and Lisa had loved the play of the multi-colored lights over Jack's glistening skin.

She never wonders about anything when they make love. Not Jamie. Not Jack's ex-wife. But when it's over and they lay together, the doubts sneak in and lay down beside her. What would it be like to make love with Jamie? Just once. And God knows that thought has gone through her mind at least five thousand and one times since Jamie offered to father her child.

Does Jack still love his ex-wife? What about his daughter? Would she like Lisa? Would she resent her?

And then last night, as she lay with her face turned to Jack's neck and his hand warm on the small of her back and the cool air kissing her sweat-dampened skin, he'd said it.

Not a big statement. Nothing sparkly and over the top. Just *I love you.*

Just *I love you.* And she'd said it back, and she meant it, but dammit all, as she'd whispered the words and pressed her lips to his neck, she'd thought of Jamie.

Just for a moment. Just to hold him. To tell him she loves him. To feel his hands caress her. To take him inside her and put her arms around him and breathe him in.

And then, guilty as if she'd said Jamie's name, she'd raised up over Jack and straddled him and taken him again and when she'd come again, she'd said *I love you* and this time she'd said *I love you, Jack,* and she'd been talking only to Jack.

So, what is she doing here? Parked in the driveway of Jamie's house, she's overwhelmed. She loves him. She hates him. She needs him. She needs to walk away from him.

Whatever it is, it needs to be acknowledged and said out loud to Jamie. Damn the torpedoes. Angie and

Makenna are right. She's lived an isosceles triangle with Brooke and Jamie for years, and one way or another, it has to stop.

She stares at Jamie and Brooke's house for a moment. A modest ranch, sand-colored siding. Two car garage. Icicle lights define the roofline the full length of the house. Festive. Ordinary. Mocking. What the hell is she afraid of?

With a deep breath, she opens her car door, climbs out, and slams the door shut. She shoves her hands in her coat pockets, uses the remote to lock the car, and hurries as best she can up the sidewalk to the front door.

As she reaches to ring the doorbell, she hopes Jamie is home. And that Brooke is not.

"Hi, Lisa," Daniel says as he opens the door. He wears that half-assed embarrassed smile that teenage boys often do. Apparently Jamie and Brooke haven't told the boys they've had a disagreement with her. Then again, what would they say? *Dad offered to father Lisa's baby, and she laughed in his face?*

"Hey, Daniel." She grins. He's a cute kid. The perfect combination of Brooke and Jamie. He has thick curly brown hair, and big green eyes. Jamie's eyes.

"C'min," Daniel tells her. She swallows hard as she steps inside, because she's picturing what a child she and Jamie might have had together thirteen years ago would look like. Would he have Jamie's eyes? Jamie's killer smile?

"Mom's out with some friends, but Dad's in the kitchen."

Lisa nods and smiles her thanks to Daniel. The kitchen. Of course. She watches Daniel walk away and head toward his room as she unbuttons her coat. There are presents under the tree in the corner, and Brooke's nativity scene is displayed on the coffee table, and it's so homey, that it breaks Lisa's heart. Again.

"Daniel?" Jamie calls. "Who was at the door?"

Lisa looks up when Jamie's voice is in the room with her. Their eyes meet across the room, but she can't hold his gaze. She looks again at the tree and tries to think about her own tree, and Jack, and making love.

"Oh."

She glances at him again, but she's blank, and she's not sure her voice would work even if she had something to say.

"Brooke went out with some friends," he tells her.

"Hey, Dad." Daniel bounds back into the living room, this time with his coat on and a duffel bag slung over his shoulder. "Brendon and his dad are out there."

"Okay." Jamie watches his son walk out the front door and yells "have fun" and then the door closes, and it's just Lisa and Jamie in the very quiet living room.

Jamie, dishtowel in hand, stares at Lisa expectantly.

She's still so full of questions and emotions and Jack and Jamie and need and love and hurt that she has no idea where to start. So much needs to be said, but at the moment, she can't think of a single thing to say.

He watches her closely, so closely she thinks he must be able to see her heart beating against her chest.

"We can't leave things like this," she finally says, and her voice is small, and her hands are shaking. "Not like this."

He doesn't answer her, and she wonders if it's too late. If this is the way things will end, and if she's welcome here or if when she walks out, she'll never set foot inside his house again.

"You're still that kid," she says carefully, "that kid that rode his bike over to my house and watched me shoot baskets. You're still the friend I wanna talk to about my day. About my students. You're still here, Jamie." She touches her heart. "And I need for us to go back to that. To that friendship. To that innocence."

"You can't take back innocence once it's gone," he answers quietly.

"We're not friends?"

He shrugs. "Maybe we really fucked things up."

"Why did you offer...what made you think..."

"That I was good enough to father your child?"

Lisa glances at the doorway again and wonders where Jared is.

"We're alone," Jamie tells her. He turns and heads back to the kitchen. Lisa follows him without an invitation.

She starts to say it isn't that he's not good enough, but he interrupts her.

"Brooke and I have talked about this a lot." His voice is flat. He's scraping something off the glass cooktop with a razor and not looking at Lisa. "I told her I think you're really in love with Jack. She said she wasn't sure, and she said she knows how much you want a family. A baby. That you want a baby with someone you love, and for some fucked-up reason, she decided I should be that someone. That we're good friends, all of us, and you and I could raise a child together."

"This was Brooke's idea?"

He shrugs. "Does it matter?"

"Kind of," she answers.

He looks at her over his shoulder.

"I thought…"

"What?" He puts the razor down and turns around to look at her. Hips against the counter, arms crossed over his chest and unreadable expression on his face, Lisa's not sure she can go on. He looks bored. Uninterested. Like he wouldn't care if she walked out and never came back.

"That it was your way of getting rid of Jack."

He stares at her for a moment and then sighs and looks away.

"If you really think that, then you and I are further apart than I thought," he mumbles.

"What do you mean?"

"It's not rocket science, Lisa."

"I don't read minds, Jamie."

"If you think I'd offer, and don't think I feel superior here, like this is the offer of a lifetime, because I don't. But if you think I'd offer to father your child just to break you and Jack up, we've got nowhere left to go."

"I still have no idea what that means," she whispers. Because can't it mean a million different things? That he wants her to be with Jack? That he doesn't? That he offered because Brooke asked him to?

That he's in love with her?

"I don't take fatherhood lightly," he snaps, and he pulls the dishtowel from his shoulder and tosses it to the counter. "Is that what you think? You think I'd go jack off in a cup to get you pregnant just to run a guy off? Am I that irresponsible, Lisa?"

Her lips part, but there's nothing she can say to that.

"I don't mean to do it," he continues, and his voice is tight and small, and Lisa knows him so well, she knows he's about to break. "I don't want you to be unhappy. You've always been…a huge part of my life. And I know… I know a lot changed when Brooke and I got married. I know that, Lisa. We changed. And I know it's not fair, but I don't want us to change more because of him."

She covers her mouth, but not before she sobs. His eyes are glassy and red.

"You have been there for me for over half my life," he tells her. "Just this beautiful person in my life. You make me laugh. You make me think. You make me a better person—"

"Jamie, that's your wife," Lisa wails. "You're not describing a friend. That's your wife."

He swallows hard and looks away from her. She watches his fingers as he rubs the dishtowel over an imaginary spot on the counter.

"There were times when we were younger, I wanted you so badly, it hurt. Some nights I thought my dick would break when I'd leave your house after we watched a movie or shot baskets. I used to dream about you."

"Then why? Why didn't you ever touch me? Tell me?"

He lifts his eyes to look at her.

"Because you always had some hot guy by the neck, leading him around. I didn't wanna get the standard *I think of you as a friend* line."

"I just wanted you," she whispers. He looks up as she wipes at her eyes. "I just wanted you."

"I never thought of you that way after I met Brooke. I love her, Lis. Brooke is my heart."

"I know that." She reaches out to touch his hand, but she stops herself. "God, I know that, Jamie."

"But since she's started in with how I should be the

one to father your child, all I can think about is you. I keep thinking about that red shirt you wear. The v-neck. The way I can see your breasts when you're sitting at your desk, and I'm talking to you. The way your legs look in your jeans, and what they would feel like wrapped around my waist. I dream—"

"Stop." She shakes her head. "God, please, stop."

"Is it that bad?" he asks her.

"What?" She backs away as he comes around the counter. He catches her wrist in his hand and pulls her back toward him. "Don't do this, Jamie."

"Would having my baby be that bad?"

The past weeks of tension and sadness rear up inside her. Twenty-five years of frustration and love and anger and tears erupt, and she drops her chin to her chest and shakes her head.

"I can't have your baby," she finally whispers. "I can't, Jamie. You're married. I need more than someone to...to make me pregnant. I need someone to love me. To hold me while I sleep. To feel the baby move, and to paint a nursery. I need the whole package, and I can't have you."

"But would you?" he asks, and the hard edge of pain in his voice makes her look up at him. "If you could, would you?"

"Why ask me? Why should I answer?" She touches him, her fingers on his face and her thumbs trace his lips. "It doesn't matter now."

She's moving before she realizes it, and then her hands slide over his face, and her fingers are in his hair, and she's touching her lips to his.

Gentle and tentative. Their first kiss is so tender, it makes her cry harder. He tastes like wine, and she wonders if he and Brooke shared a bottle over dinner, and for just a moment she hates Brooke and she presses her body to his and God, she loves him.

"Lisa." He breaks the kiss, and she's cold, and it can't be over, and then he kisses her again. Harder. Desperately. His hands roam over her back and cup her butt, and he lifts her, and she wraps her legs around him, and the kiss burns her. He's hard against her middle, and she wants him inside her.

Just once.

"I can't," she says and she hates herself. "I can't, Jamie. I can't do this."

"I need you."

"No, you don't," she answers. "You need me out of here. Out of your life. You're married. You're happy. I can't do this."

"She knows how much I need you."

Lisa shakes her head. Hands on his chest, she pushes him away and wiggles until he sets her down.

"I won't do this to you or your family."

He nods. "I'm sorry."

"Don't be," she says softly. "I've wanted to kiss you like that for twenty-five years."

She turns and walks out of the kitchen. She's not whole. She'll never be whole again, because her heart is at Jamie's feet.

She looks back and sees that he's followed her, and he's watching her put her coat on. He's broken, and it kills her that she's done this to him. That they've broken each other.

"Jamie," she says, and she rushes to him. Her fingers on

his face again. Caressing him. Her thumb over his open lips. His breath on her skin.

She leans into him and presses her lips over his in a soft kiss. And she gives him everything. Everything she is is on her lips, and she puts them on his, and their last kiss is so sad.

"I love you," she whispers. "I've always loved you, and that's why I can't do this."

He is still broken, but he nods. He stands a little taller, and Lisa wonders if just her confession might have fixed him. Just a small part of him, maybe.

"I love you, too, Lisa." He kisses her hand and lets go and steps back from her. "Always will."

She smiles, even though she's still crying, and then she turns and walks away from him and out the door and wonders again if this is it or if they can move on now that it's all been said.

Because she loves him.

And he's still her best friend.

ngie

LISA LOOKS LIKE HELL. HUNGOVER, LIKE SHE WAS HELL-bent on drinking herself to death last night. Her eyes are swollen, and her face is streaked with makeup. She's wearing sweatpants and a t-shirt, and it's obvious she slept in them and the streaked makeup.

She knows without a word that their annual Christmas Eve Eve lunch isn't going to happen. It's already noon, and it might take a good year or two to make Lisa presentable. Besides, Lisa's obviously not up for it.

Lisa just shakes her head, but Makenna takes her coat off and tosses it on the couch.

"Go take a shower. I'll make you some breakfast."

"I'm not hungover. Just had a rough night."

"How rough?" Angie asks.

"Cried myself to sleep," Lisa admits. "Which I haven't done since high school, and I'm not proud of myself."

Makenna, who is taking her boots off, looks up quickly.

"What happened?"

"Not what you think, and that's not what I meant," Lisa answers. "I'm not gonna be good company, so go without me."

"What happened?" Angie repeats.

"I went to see Jamie last night," Lisa answers. "God, my head hurts."

"C'mon." Makenna puts her arm around Lisa's shoulders and walks her to the kitchen. Angie finally unzips her coat and steps out of her shoes. "You want coffee, Ang?"

"No," Angie answers Makenna. "Thanks."

Lisa sits at the round, wooden kitchen table with her head in her hands. Makenna makes her coffee like she owns the place. Angie helps herself to a glass of iced tea.

"Spill." Makenna nudges Lisa's shoulder.

"It's all been said," Lisa says quietly.

"And done?" Angie asks as she sits down at the table with Lisa.

"Is that what you really think of me?"

"I think you've been very much in love with him for a really long time, and I think he feels the same way about you. And if you did spend the night together, I think I'd understand."

Lisa rubs her face and then drags her fingers back through her hair. Angie tries to imagine it. Lisa going to see Jamie. Maybe no one was home. Maybe the boys were downstairs. Maybe they got in a shouting match. Maybe one of them grabbed the other, and maybe a kiss started it, and maybe things got out of hand.

She hopes it didn't happen that way. But she *would* understand.

"It's human nature," she adds.

Lisa shakes her head. "No. It didn't happen."

"Then what did happen?"

Lisa jumps when her phone rings. She glances at it, and Makenna picks up the cordless handset.

"It's Jack," she says as she looks at the caller ID.

Lisa shakes her head. "Let it go."

"Lisa?"

"I can't talk to him right now."

Angie and Makenna glance at each other, but neither of them says anything. Makenna sets the phone down and goes back to the counter. She opens a cabinet, takes out a bottle of aspirin, and shakes two out for Lisa.

"I don't have a hangover," Lisa repeats. "I didn't drink anything last night."

"You said you had a headache," Makenna reminds her.

Lisa nods. Makenna gets her a glass of juice and then sits down with them at the table.

"Look, it's okay." Lisa swallows the pills with the orange juice. "It's fine. There's no big rift in the cosmos. Jamie's still married. I'm still dating Jack. We just played our cards last night." Lisa shrugs.

"Who won?" Angie asks softly.

Lisa shakes her head. "Draw."

Angie doesn't have the energy for this. To draw Lisa out. It's like pulling teeth these days, getting Lisa to talk, and she's not up for it, so frustration boils inside her.

"I went over to his house," Lisa begins, and Angie wonders if she's wearing that frustration on her face. "I couldn't leave things like they were. Figured it was time for all or nothing."

"Good." Angie nods.

Lisa smiles, but her eyes fill suddenly, and then tears streak her face. "Yeah, good. Turns out he's always loved me, but he was afraid to say so when we were younger. Afraid I would say I just wanted to be friends."

Lisa blinks, even as she continues to cry. "And now, of course, he loves Brooke, and I wouldn't have it any other way. But God, the years we wasted. Things could be so different."

"Did you tell him?" Angie asks.

Lisa sits back and draws her knees up to her chest. She drags her knuckles under her eyes and nods. "I did. I kissed him." She smiles and looks first at Angie and then at Makenna. "Our affair lasted about ten minutes. An incredible kiss in the kitchen. I felt completely naked in his arms." She licks her lips and shrugs and stares at her juice glass on the table. "I wanted to be naked in his arms."

"I'm so sorry," Makenna whispers, and Angie realizes she's on the verge of tears herself.

"I couldn't do it," Lisa says and shakes her head. "I'm not a home-wrecker. Especially not Jamie's. I said no. I mean, maybe he would've said the same if I hadn't. But I said no," she continues. "And I walked away."

Angie tries to imagine loving Brian as she does, but knowing she can't have him. Loving him for a lifetime, while he is off-limits.

"But I looked back," Lisa cries. "And he just…looked so lost. And it hurt so much."

"Lisa." Angie touches Lisa's hand.

"I kissed him goodbye. And told him I had to walk away, because I loved him."

Makenna brushes at the tears on her face.

"And he said he loved me too, and then I left. And I came home, and I curled up in bed, and I thought about everything I could have had with Jamie, and I cried." Lisa stands up and turns on the kitchen faucet. Angie watches her reach for the dishwashing liquid and squirt some in the sink.

"The nights we could have made love. Babies we may have had," Lisa says. "Christmas trees decorated with our child's pictures. And the whole time I was thinking that, I was thinking about Brooke and Jack, and I hated myself but I couldn't stop. I mean, it has to be this way. Jamie's married, and I have Jack. And I want Jack. I want him in my life."

Angie gets up and turns the faucet off. There are no dishes to wash, other than the juice glass on the table. She leads Lisa back to the table.

"I can't have Jamie's baby. I don't want to have a child with someone who couldn't be there every day. Who wouldn't love me, other than because I'm the mother of his child. I don't know. Maybe things will go that way for me and Jack. Who knows? How can anybody know? It just has to happen—"

"Lisa." Makenna says firmly, and Lisa stops and looks at Makenna as if she's surprised to see her sitting there.

"I mean, I'm okay, guys. It's better this way. Better for all of us. Maybe there's a process for this. Like the twelve steps or something. For missed opportunities. It just hurts."

"Of course, it hurts," Angie agrees.

"The really stupid thing?" Lisa raises her eyebrows. "I waited to do this until after Jack said he loved me. We were here the night before. Had dinner together. A bottle of wine. Watched a movie together. Made love. And then he said it. And it was so sincere. It was everything I thought I wanted. And when I said it to him, I meant it."

Angie and Makenna chance another look at each other.

"And then the next night, I go back to my poison. Does that make me a bitch or what?"

"It makes you human," Makenna says gently.

"It makes you a woman desperately in love with someone she can't have."

Lisa takes a deep breath.

"I'm so proud of you, Lisa. For talking to Jamie. For being honest with yourself and with Jamie."

"Forgive me, Ang, but right now your pride doesn't mean dick-all to me."

"I know," Angie says and then they laugh.

"Don't get me wrong. I'm not pining away for him. I feel more like someone died. We put it to rest last night."

Angie nods, and she thinks she knows what Lisa is going to say next.

"I don't know where we go from here. Me and Jack. Me and Jamie. Do I have the right to be with Jack if I haven't been honest with him about Jamie? Can Jamie and I carry our friendship forward and leave everything else alone?"

Lisa looks to Angie, but Angie just shakes her head.

"I don't know, Lisa. I don't know about you and Jamie. But you and Jack have time to figure things out."

"Have you ever kissed your best friend, with your heart and soul and been able to look him in the eye the next day and pretend it never happened?"

"Considering you two are my best friends," Makenna says, "no."

They laugh, and then Lisa laughs and cries. "I'm hungry. Guess I'm human. Last night I thought I'd never eat again."

"Whaddaya want?" Makenna asks. "I'll fix something—"

"No." Lisa rubs her eyes and pulls in another deep breath. "Life goes on. Gimme a half hour, tops. We'll go out."

They sit at the kitchen table and avoid each other's eyes until Lisa disappears, and they hear the shower running.

"Long time coming," Makenna mumbles.

"No win situation."

"Maybe that remains to be seen."

Angie stands and lets the water out of the kitchen sink. She rinses the juice glass and puts it in the dishwasher.

"I think Brooke forced their hands."

"I don't know if I'd be so ready to gamble my marriage that way," Makenna says thoughtfully.

"Wouldn't you? I would've put money on Lisa doing the right thing."

Makenna shrugs and heads to the living room. Angie follows her and watches when she turns the tree lights on.

"But who's to say walking away was the right thing?"

Angie can't believe she heard Makenna right. She shakes her head.

"Huh-uh, Kenna. This is it. It's over. We have to stop thinking that way, because Lisa did the right thing."

"Ten minutes with the love of her life."

"She's strong," Angie says firmly. "She'll be fine."

Angie hopes Makenna can't see through her and know that she's bluffing. Lisa might be fine with Jack. They might have a future. They might be happy.

But what happens the first time Lisa and Jamie come face to face after giving each other everything in one kiss?

All or nothing, Angie thinks, and she turns away from Makenna to look at the tree and wonder just what it would look like if it were Lisa and Jamie's tree.

27

L isa

LISA IS AWAKE AT SIX-THIRTY IN THE MORNING ON
Christmas Eve. She has no desire to get up, but she's wide
awake, so she stays in bed and thinks, remembers the way
Christmas made her feel when she was a kid. The way
each day leading up to Christmas seemed to last two days,
and the last week seemed to take a year all by itself. Her
Christmases hadn't ever been quite like Angie or Makenna's, but her dad had done okay by her until she was old
enough to take care of herself.

They'd always gone to dinner and a movie on
Christmas Eve. Just the two of them. At least it *had* just
been the two of them; he'd never brought another woman
into the picture when Lisa was younger. Although that

may be why his moving away and getting married and having another child had been such a blow to the adult Lisa.

They'd open presents Christmas morning, and then he would fix breakfast. And sometimes Lisa would leave and go to church with Angie or Makenna's family. Lisa finds herself missing her dad and the days when she lived at home.

She hasn't talked to Jamie since that night. It's probably for the best. She's not ready to talk to him, though she hopes that someday soon she will be. That someday soon he'll be ready to talk to her. As precious as those moments in his arms were, she's not entirely sure she should have traded them for twenty-five years of friendship.

She desperately hopes that it wasn't really a trade.

Her phone rings, and she looks at the clock. Her heartbeat quickens, because no one calls her house before seven o'clock, especially on the morning of Christmas Eve, unless there is something wrong.

"Hello?"

"Lisa."

It's Jack. She sags back into her pillow, but then she wonders why he's calling her so early, and it occurs to her that he may be calling to break their plans to spend the evening together, to spend tomorrow together.

"Hey." She can't say more, because the thought of not being with Jack today fills her with sadness.

"I'm laying here awake, thinking about you," he says. "And wondering why we can't start our Christmas together right now. Instead of later this afternoon."

"Come." Her voice is thick with tears. "Come now."

And he's there within a half hour, and she leads him back to her bed. They sleep till nine, after they make love, and she awakens to feel his warm, hard body curled around her.

She stretches and pushes back into him. He slides his hand over her hip and leans over to press a kiss to her neck, just below her ear.

"Jack?"

"Hmm?"

"I'm hungry." She laughs, and then he laughs and tugs her over to lie on her back.

"Me, too."

"No, really. Like bacon and eggs hungry."

"Me, too."

It takes them twenty minutes to untangle themselves and dress and move out of the bedroom. She makes coffee while he makes omelets. And then, since it's Christmas Eve, she thinks they should have a treat, a little something more than what they've just shared in her bedroom. So, she mixes muffins, and her house smells like cinnamon, and finally feeling something inside other than empty, she turns on a Christmas CD and for a minute, she remembers the night she, Makenna, and Angie had decorated her tree.

She's glad they made her put the tree up. Her house feels festive for the first time since she's moved here. It feels lived in, cozy. The tree lights are on, and there are several presents under the tree. She and Jack are making breakfast together, and they have plans for the evening and tomorrow.

And maybe the day after that.

"Thank you," she says when he pours her a mug of coffee.

"You make me happy," he tells her as he slips his arms around her waist.

"Me, too." She rubs her hands up his arms and lets them rest on his shoulders.

"Do you ever wonder where we're going? With this?" He nods his head at her as if to say us.

"I do," she answers. "But I'm not in any hurry."

He nods and lowers his head to kiss her.

"There's a lot," she breaks the kiss and looks up at him, afraid to get into this but knowing she has to, "we've never talked about. Things we don't know about each other."

"We don't have to be in a hurry."

She nods and lays her head on his shoulder.

"But I do want to ask you something."

Her heart punches so hard inside her she wonders if he feels it.

"What?"

She doesn't want to know, because she can't imagine anything he asks her being good. She sure isn't ready for the Big Question, as much as she wishes she were. She doesn't want to dredge up old relationships today, most certainly not with her most recent loss. Then again, that wasn't exactly a relationship.

"What're you doing New Year's Eve?"

She laughs, but her eyes fill, and she thinks how she's been crying at the drop of a hat and how ridiculous it is.

"Because whatever it is, I wanna be there with you," Jack tells her, "so we can ring in the new year together. I wanna start the new year with you."

She nods. "I don't know what I'm doing," she answers. "I think I might still be standing right here in your arms. And that'll be perfect."

"It's a date."

Later, after breakfast is eaten, and the kitchen is clean, and they've showered and dressed, they head out in Jack's car to the mall. They need nothing, but Lisa loves just strolling the mall, hand in hand with him. They talk about everything and nothing, and the Christmas music that plays from store to store swells inside her, until she feels like she could float. They see several of their students, some with family and some with friends, and laugh at the looks of surprise on their faces.

It's official now. Every student and parent will know before Christmas Day that Miss Fairchild is dating Mr. Holloman. And she doesn't care. No, actually that's not true. She's glad. She's ready to let the world know she's lost her heart to someone.

No, that's not right either. She hasn't lost her heart. She's *given* it to someone.

They share a plate of nachos and drink a beer around four, at the bar and grill in the mall. And then as they walk back down the mall, thinking they could go to an early movie (after all, mass doesn't start until ten), Jack yanks her to the window of the Fire and Ice Jewelry store.

"What're you doing?" she asks him, and she laughs, but the nachos and the beer are beginning to twist in her stomach. She thought they'd covered this stuff earlier today.

"Just looking," he tells her. "Someday...new year..."

"Jack?"

He stands up straight and looks her in the eye.

"Okay, I know earlier we said we don't have to rush. And I'm not rushing. I'm just letting you know this is what I'm thinking about. For someday."

"Someday."

"Mm-hmm."

"But not New Year's Day?"

"No." He squeezes her hand and laughs quietly. "No. I just meant someday, in a new year."

She nods, and when a bouncy little blonde comes over and asks Jack if he needs any help, he barely glances at the girl and says no, that they're just looking.

"So. You've thought about this? About rings and getting married again?"

He nods. "I have."

"You've thought about marrying me?"

"I have."

But what about your ex-wife? she wants to say. What about your daughter? I haven't even met her. What about having other children? She even opens her mouth, but she stops herself. He's thought about it.

She's thought about it.

No promises. No hurries.

"Have you?" he asks her as they walk hand in hand away from the window.

"Have I what?"

"Thought about it? Marrying me?"

Suddenly she feels a little shy, and she simply grins and nods. It's all so new to her. And yet, she knows she must tread lightly, because of what's just happened between her and Jamie. The fastest way to hurt everyone involved would be to rush into something with Jack before she's ready.

"So. Maybe someday?"

She laughs and remembers girls in high school who wore tiny diamond rings and said they were pre-engaged. She wonders if this is how their pre-proposals went.

"Yeah. Maybe. Someday."

ngie

SHE THINKS OF IT AS MIDNIGHT MASS, THOUGH THE MASS begins at ten and is actually over by midnight. She has gone to this Christmas mass as far back as she can remember. Each year the group varies, but usually there are several members of her family here, and Makenna's family sits close by, and Brooke and Jamie are usually here, and Lisa is always with someone.

Angie kind of worries about the whole Lisa and Jamie thing, but, it's Christmas Eve, and she doesn't want to. It's time to let it go and let the pieces fall where they may.

It's so damned cold outside that she'd felt that twinge as she and Piper had walked, arm in arm, into the dimly-lit, cavernous church. They had dinner at her dad's house. She and Piper had fixed most of it, but her dad had made the dressing, and she's glad. Not only because it's delicious, but also because she likes to see him keeping busy. Presents and games and movies and fudge and cookies filled the day, and Angie knows tomorrow will be more of the same.

It's fun, but it's not. It's the end. Again. Just exactly as Makenna had said awhile back. Christmas is everything that leads up to the big day, and then in twenty-four hours, it's over. It gets harder to put it all back on the shelves each year and face a stark, cold January.

She'd been so tired when they got home from her dad's. So cold. She'd sat by the fire for a moment and started to doze off, and then Brian was there, shaking her and saying that it was time to change for mass.

And so now, here she is with Piper, half-wishing she was at home in bed. Except that she loves the church on this night. When it's quiet and semi-dark, and the trees decorate the altar, and the manger scene is at the side altar. She loves this part of Christmas, and so as she and Piper genuflect and sit in the pew where her dad already sits by her uncle, she feels that hard spot inside her begin to melt away.

Makenna and Dave and the girls sit in front of them, and Angie reaches over the pew to hug Makenna.

"Merry Christmas," she whispers.

"You, too."

The musicians are warming up, and Angie says a silent prayer of thanks for these particular musicians because she needs the music to enjoy the mass. Four men: one plays the piano, two play the guitar and one sings. So simple and so perfect.

Angie scoots over when Brian and Zach genuflect.

Brooke and Jamie and the boys come into the church from the front door. Angie watches them closely, and then she wonders what she's looking for. Jamie's not an adulterer; there won't be a letter A on his chest any more than there would be on Lisa's. But, he lost something that night, too, and she wonders if it will show in him as it does in Lisa.

He looks good, though, in his charcoal gray suit and green Christmas tie. Damned good, and suddenly Angie is worried about Lisa again. But Jamie's eyes meet hers as he waits for his family to slide into the pew in front of Makenna and Dave's.

He starts to smile, but it catches, and he's frozen, and Angie almost feels him asking for forgiveness. For betraying his wife with a kiss? For betraying his friendship with a kiss? For hurting Lisa? She doesn't know, but she sees the sorrow in his eyes and the lost sleep in the lines around his eyes, and it breaks her heart that her friends are hurting.

She smiles at him, and she hopes he sees that there is nothing to forgive. It doesn't concern her, because it's about Jamie and Lisa, and yet it does concern her, because they're both her friends. But no one's in the wrong, as far as she can tell.

Actually, as Lisa had said the other day, they'd put it to rest. And maybe next year at this time, they will look back on this and be relieved to have it done.

Makenna looks over her shoulder, and suddenly her eyes are wide like maybe Santa Claus has just walked in. Angie turns to see what she's staring at, and she sees Lisa. With Jack.

Lisa is stunning in winter white slacks and a black

sweater and her long black leather coat. Jack, whom Angie has only seen once or twice, wears a black suit, with a white shirt and red tie. They're smiling, and they hold hands, and they look to all the world as if they are a happy, solid couple, and Angie prays that they are.

They sit in the pew behind Angie's family, and Lisa leans forward and hugs Angie hard and presses a kiss to her cheek.

"Merry Christmas," she says as she wipes the smudge of lipstick away with her thumb, and Angie says Merry Christmas, and she smiles at Jack. He's good-looking, that's for sure. Angie wonders how this will play out when mass is over. Will Lisa stick around and talk to everyone? To Jamie?

But there isn't time to wonder long, because mass starts, and the congregation stands, and they sing "Joy to the World." She sits with her arm around Piper through the mass, and she listens to Father's homily about God's promise and loving the world and forgiveness.

Love and forgiveness, she thinks. After Communion, the lights are dimmed again, and the ushers pass out candles to those at the ends of the pews. When they are lit, everyone sings "Silent Night," and Angie looks around. She looks at her dad, and she knows that maybe someday she'll lose him, but he's here now, and he's healthy. She looks at her husband, and she thanks God that she and Brian have each other and have never had to work around obstacles to be together. She looks at her friends, and she thinks of the past season and of how a few times she was so exhausted that she was ready to cut them all loose and walk away.

The tears that never came at the Christmas program

suddenly burn in her eyes. This is Christmas. Christmas is love. Christmas is the big stuff, the Nativity, the advent wreath, the hours of decorating and shopping and wrapping. And Christmas is the little stuff. So much magic so entwined and entangled in all the big stuff that it might take forever to name it all.

The way the tree itself speaks to her before it's even decorated. Snitching cookie dough while Piper rolls it out to use the cookie cutters. The perfect paper and gift tags for her kids. Ribbing Makenna about her Christmas music addiction. The North Pole and hot chocolate and Spoons.

The small hours they've all spent together.

She swallows hard, because her throat has gone tight, and she blinks hard, because she doesn't want anyone to know that she's standing here crying a mix of happy and sad tears.

When mass is over, Angie hugs her aunts and uncles, and they promise they'll see each other tomorrow, and they will. Even after that flood of emotion just a moment ago, Angie feels that pang again about tomorrow. Christmas.

The end of Christmas.

She looks up when her family is gone, except for Brian and the kids, and she sees Lisa and Jack standing with Brooke and Jamie. Brian puts his arm around her and pulls her close and says close to her ear, "They'll be okay."

She's told Brian everything, because she always tells Brian everything and because he never repeats the things she shares. She trusts him completely, and so when he says they'll be okay, she believes him. She moves slowly out of the pew and decides it is better not to bother them, but then Lisa calls softly to them.

"Ang, Makenna, this is Jack," she tells them, and then she looks at Jack and says, "these are my other best friends, Angie Edwards and Makenna Hodges."

Jack's handshake is firm, and he's friendly, and he says he's pleased to meet them. But in her mind, Angie is hearing how Lisa said her other best friends, and so probably she'd introduced Jamie to Jack as her best friend.

That's good, Angie thinks, but she wonders if that was a blow to Jamie. Except it doesn't matter, because Jamie's married, and they settled this, and now here Angie's the one making herself crazy over the whole thing again.

Jamie is smiling, and Angie doesn't want to stare too hard. But it seems real. He has his arm around Brooke, and she seems happy, and Angie decides either it's okay, or everyone involved has a hell of a poker face.

29

J amie

IF IT WERE UP TO HIM, THEY WOULD GO TO AN EARLIER mass. And that has nothing to do with Lisa. At least it's never had anything to do with Lisa until now. The last month has thrown a wrench in the wheels, and at least inside him, all hell broke loose, and it's still shifting inside.

He loves Brooke, and he has no intention of losing her. No plans to put the moves on Lisa, but now sometimes he thinks about her. In ways that he shouldn't. He'd cried when she left that night. When she'd told him no and walked away from him. When she'd kissed him goodbye and said she loved him and left. Just silent tears, and then that had pissed him off, so he'd gone downstairs and gone an hour on the treadmill and beat the hell out of his boxing bag. He was so sore the next morning he could hardly move. He hadn't worked out in God knows how long, and he'd lied to Brooke about being sore. He'd lied about it, and it was simple and innocent, and yet he'd lied, and lying had made him feel so damned guilty.

He'd steeled himself for tonight. For seeing Lisa. But he hadn't been prepared to see her with Jack. Looking like the damned queen and king of marital bliss. They were fluid, and they moved together. They walked in step, and Jack touched her back possessively as they walked up to talk to him and Brooke. He was a good-looking guy, and probably if Lisa weren't involved with him, Jamie would think he was an okay guy.

Lisa looks incredible, he thinks now. She's full of life and energy, and it shocks him a little that she can look so happy, so full after the other night. Because he'd felt drained. And half-dead when the front door had closed on any unspoken possibility they'd ever had.

He's an idiot, and he knows that. His wife had almost handed him another woman, and not just any other woman, but the other love of his life. Hell, who knows. Maybe Brooke had done it to test him. He'd passed, in the flesh anyway, but he was still struggling with the rest of it. He'd been an idiot to consider it. What did he expect? Had he thought Lisa would want to carry his baby? That maybe it would lead to something more? Or had he just lost all rational thought the second she'd put her mouth on his and pressed her body against his? And now he's what? Pissed? Disappointed? Frustrated? Because for just a second, he'd been a total ass and thought he was going to have it all.

One night of passion and love with his other woman?

And then back to being happily married the next day? Like that wasn't going to hurt Brooke. Or Lisa.

So mostly, maybe, he's pissed at himself. For his raging hormones and his mental vacation and the fact that he's still thinking about it. Still thinking about undressing her and taking her there in the kitchen.

He reminds himself that he's in a church, and the last thing he needs is God to strike him dead with lightning in the middle of the winter, in the middle of a church. Because then wouldn't just about everybody here know just exactly what he was thinking? They're saying good-bye, and it occurs to him he hasn't said jack to Lisa or Jack, and she probably thinks he's being a dick. Again. Still. But he's not. Not this time. He's treading water. Fair and square.

He mumbles *goodbye* and *it was nice to meet you*, and then Lisa and Jack turn, and they're walking away, and Jamie wonders if this will always stand in the way of their friendship. Apparently Lisa has gotten over it already, because she's here with Jack, and she'd introduced Jamie as her best friend, and she'd done so with a steady, strong voice. No hint of the raw emotion she'd given him the other night.

Let it go, Maczum, he tells himself. But then he looks up, and Lisa rushes back to him. She throws her arms around him and kisses his cheek and says *Merry Christmas*.

"Merry Christmas, Lisa," he says, and he holds her tight, and then he lets her go.

30

L isa

CHRISTMAS DAY HAD BEEN SO DIFFERENT FOR HER. SHE'D shared the whole day with Jack. He'd stayed over at her house Christmas Eve, and they'd stayed in bed until after nine Christmas morning. Breakfast together again. They'd exchanged gifts; Lisa had been speechless when she'd opened the diamond pendant necklace from Jack. He'd seemed pleased with the scarf and sweater she'd given him, though she'd felt a little guilty after his extravagant gift.

She'd called her dad, and even though Jack sat beside her while she talked to him, she didn't tell her dad about him. Not yet. Not because she wasn't sure about Jack. Because she didn't feel close enough to her dad to want to share anything about him. Maybe someday.

He'd called his daughter, and he'd only talked to his ex-wife for a moment, and Lisa couldn't detect anything more than polite interest in his voice. He didn't tell his daughter about her, and she was okay with that. There would be time.

They'd gone to Makenna's house for dinner, and they'd fit right in with her family. Jack had played games with the girls and watched TV with Dave while she and Makenna and her cousins did the dishes.

Jack had gone home a time or two during the holidays, but he'd always come back to her house. Maybe it wasn't proper for him to be spending his nights there, since they weren't married (what would their students think?), but he was always careful to pull his car into the garage.

Lisa watches Makenna and Piper play tennis on the Wii. It is after ten on New Year's Eve, and they are at Angie's. The house is packed, and Lisa wonders if Makenna feels at all possessive of Angie. There are other friends here, people Angie knows from work and parents of Piper's friends and Zach's friends and even people Brian works with, and Lisa can't help but feel put out, because Angie belongs to her and Makenna.

She takes a drink of her wine. Piper is amazing. She's becoming a woman, and the thought makes Lisa think again about babies, and she wonders if it's too late. If she should let that dream go.

Makenna and Piper are cracking up, and now Angie and Daniel are playing Just Dance, and suddenly Jamie is standing by her.

"Hey."

"Hi."

He looks tired, and he's aged in the last couple of

weeks, and Lisa knows she put some of those lines in his face. Then again, how many nights of sleep did she lose over him through the years?

"You look so happy," he says quietly. He smiles, and it's that smile that's always been just for her. "Tell me you're happy."

Who can ever be happy without a twinge of sadness, she wonders, and someone must be dicking with them, because the music that's playing rolls smoothly into Dan Fogelberg's song "Same Auld Lang Syne."

She kind of laughs, but she knows it misses its mark. Jamie notices the song, too.

"Great. Cheesey seventies stuff. I thought we might rate better than this."

"I like this song," she says. "I'm happy, Jamie. I'm really happy."

He nods. "Good." She watches as he pours her more wine, and then he lifts his own glass in a toast to hers. "What comes after innocence?"

"Truth?" she suggests.

He stares at her for a moment, and finally, he nods.

"To truth."

They touch glasses and then drink, and then Jamie leans over and drops a quick kiss on her lips and walks away. She watches him and sees that he's talking to Jared now.

"There's a story there, isn't there?" Jack says quietly, and she turns to find him standing by her.

"A short story, maybe," she answers, and she smiles sadly. "Stay by me."

"Why?" he asks. He puts his arms around her. A grin tugs at the corners of his mouth.

"Because I need to practice kissing you for midnight."

"You don't need a bit of practice, Lisa Fairchild."

"Happy New Year, Jack." She leans into him and lays her head on his chest.

"It's not the new year yet, babe."

"It is for me," she answers. And she kisses him, like the ball is dropping, and the year is new, and she's ready. She's ready for the new year with Jack.

And maybe someday...

"Lisa!" Angie calls from across the basement. "Get your ass over here."

"I'm celebrating."

"Let's play tennis."

Lisa looks up at Jack. He smiles and nods. "Go. I'll be right here."

ABOUT THE AUTHOR

Tracy is the author of the Lorelei Bluffs women's fiction series, the Williams Legacy—also a women's fiction series — and several stand-alone women's fiction novels, including Damsel. She also writes contemporary romance and is the author of The Mississippi Queen Trilogy and other stand-alone romance novels.

When not writing, Tracy enjoys traveling, reading, and spending time with family. She lives in the Midwest with her husband of twenty-six years, two mostly grown-up kids, and two dachshunds, who might be more spoiled than the kids.

To learn more about Tracy and her work, visit her online at www.broemmerbooks.com

ALSO BY TRACY BROEMMER

Women's Fiction Novels:

Luther's Cross (Writing as Therese Kinkaide)

Luther's Cross 10th Anniversary Edition (Tracy Broemmer)

Fairytale (Writing as Therese Kinkaide)

Just Like Them (Writing as Therese Kinkaide)

Picket Fences

Two Story Home

Green-Eyed Girl

Say Everything

Come Home For Christmas

Sketching Litchfield Lake

Ever, Again

Safe as Houses

Damsel

Every Little Thing, Lorelei Bluffs, Book 1

Two A.M., Lorelei Bluffs, Book 2

Blind, Lorelei Bluffs, Book 3

Leaving July, Lorelei Bluffs, Book 4

Hesitation Marks, Lorelei Bluffs, Book 5

Four Letter Words, Lorelei Bluffs, Book 6

See Kate, Lorelei Bluffs, Book 7

Loved You More, Lorelei Bluffs, Book 8

A Lorelei Ending, Lorelei Bluffs, Book 9

I Do, Lorelei Bluffs, Book 10

Truth Is, The Williams Legacy, Book 1

Other People's Ugly, The Williams Legacy, Book 2

Omissions, The Williams Legacy, Book 3

Contemporary Romance Novels:

Destiny's Calling: Your Future Is Waiting

Wedding Day Shenanigans

Holiday Fling

The Kiss Off

Something Like Love

Love, Nashville, The Mississippi Queen Trilogy, Book 1

Forever, Duncan, The Mississippi Queen Trilogy, Book 2

Always, Jess, The Mississippi Queen Trilogy, Book 3

Gettin' Hitched, The H Books, Book 1

Contemporary Romance Novellas:

Indian Summer, A Novella

Dear Jaclyn Perris, A Novella

Contemporary Romance Short Stories:

Perfect Pictures, The Wine Tasting Series, Traminette

Coming Home, The Wine Tasting Series, Edelweiss

Save Me Every Dance, The Wine Tasting Series, Rosé

Marry Me, The Wine Tasting Series, Shiraz

Birthday Wishes, The Wine Tasting Series, Muscat

Dad Jeans, The Wine Tasting Series, Vignoles